Issue No. 33

Winter 2022

PULP LITERATURE PRESS
Issue No. 33, Winter 2022

Publisher: Pulp Literature Press; Managing Editor: Jennifer Landels; Senior Editor: Mel Anastasiou; Acquisitions Editor: Genevieve Wynand; Poetry Editors: Daniel Cowper & Emily Osborne; Assistant Editors: Samantha Olson, Brooklynn Hook, Veronika Kos, Melisa Gruger; Copy Editors: Amanda Bidnall, Mary Rykov; Proofreader: Mary Rykov; Graphic Design: Amanda Bidnall; Cover Design: Kate Landels; First Readers: Carol McCauley, Jessica Fabrizius, Jeya Thiessen; Subscriptions: Carol McCauley; Advertising: Samantha Olson. For advertising rates, direct inquiries to info@pulpliterature.com.

Cover painting, *Space Cat* by Bronwyn Schuster. Artwork for 'Sap & Seed' by Dante Luiz. All other illustrations by Mel Anastasiou.

Pulp Literature: ISSN 2292-2164 (Print), ISSN 2292-2172 (Digital), Issue No. 33, Winter 2022.

Pulp Literature Press gratefully acknowledges the support of the Canada Council for the Arts.

Canada Council Conseil des arts
for the Arts du Canada

Pulp Literature is a proud member of the Magazine Association of BC and Magazines Canada.

TABLE OF CONTENTS

FROM THE PULP LIT PULPIT

A Walk in the Words

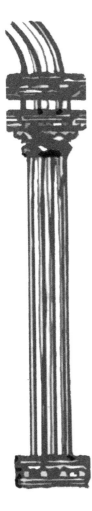

Recently I learned that *holoholo* is the Hawaiian word for walking with no destination in mind. A delightful experience, that. Setting forth on a journey with no predetermined endpoint, meandering through one's thoughts according to whatever push or pull arises, not knowing what waits on the flip side of the next leaf ... Sounds a bit like reading, doesn't it?

Or maybe reading is more of an 'all roads lead to Rome' situation: *mille viae ducunt homines per sæcula Romam.* Literally, 'a thousand roads lead people through the centuries to Rome'. No matter the path we choose, no matter our navigation, so long as we keep walking, we will, somehow, arrive.

A *sæculum* is the length of time equivalent to one's potential lifetime. It is a connection to those who've come before us and to those who will come after. Whichever of the thousand roads we choose, we journey to the centre of things—and to ourselves and to each other. Reading helps with that, too.

There are clues to the mystery everywhere. The short sound of the first letter of the English language is that of a sigh. A sigh of relief, perhaps, or of recognition or sadness or joy. You take one breath, and then another, and then — big release. Another of reading's offerings.

To journey with books is to travel through love and loss, pleasure and pain, innocence and experience, disillusionment and (if we're lucky) awakening. We encounter what Zorba, in *Zorba the Greek*, refers to as 'the full catastrophe': in reading, and reading widely, we confront and embrace it all. *Big-breath reading*, you might say.

May the stories in your life catch your breath — and may they take it away.

~*Genevieve Wynand*

In THIS ISSUE

A giant feline swats us into the void with 'Space Cat' by **Bronwyn Schuster**. And feature author **Kate Heartfield** leads us on a daring escape through the universe in 'And in the Arcade, Ego'.

Hitch a ride into the heat — and heart — of the desert with **Kevin Sandefur's** 'Out in the Sticks'. And it all goes up in flames in 'Paper, Candles, Hearts and Other Combustible Materials' by **Anne Baldo**.

Natalie Harris-Spencer in 'The Art of Ironing' and **Cara Waterfall** in 'Vessel' illustrate ways of navigating relationships and bodily autonomy. And friendship transcends time and place in 'Fate of Chickens' by **Krista Jane May**.

We delve into familial grief and sacrifice in 'Sap and Seed' by **H Pueyo** and **Dante Luiz** and the opening chapters of 'Allaigna's Song: Chorale' by **JM Landels**, while 'Pale Pony Express' by **Lulu Keating** and 'The echo of light footsteps on parchment' by **Kimberley Aslett** explore memory and loss through storytelling.

Strange science brings us 'The Magic Shuffling Machine' by **Derek Salinas Lazarski** but can't explain the tiny home intruder in 'The Switch Fairy' by **Monica Wang** or the supernatural occurrences in 'Pretty Lies: Eyes Full of Moon' by **Mel Anastasiou**.

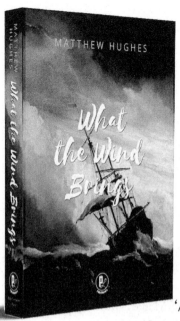

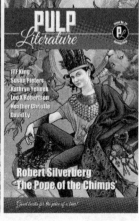

AND IN THE ARCADE, EGO

Kate Heartfield

Kate Heartfield *is the author of* The Embroidered Book, *a historical fantasy novel to be released in February 2022. Her debut novel won Canada's Aurora Award, and her novellas, stories, and games have been shortlisted for the Nebula, Locus, Crawford, Sunburst, and Aurora awards. A former journalist, Kate lives near Ottawa, Canada.*

$\mathcal{A}$ND IN THE ARCADE, EGO

Luz torches the Fugax right after we roll out of it, before I even hit the floor of the landing bay. She lights it up like an offering with one of her chemical grenades, holding on to a bay-grip with one hand, and kicks the speedcraft, all sparking and spinning, out into space.

I cringe when it explodes. The smoothest ride around, so pretty and sleek. Worth more denari than I'll make in my lifetime. But Luz just pumps one fist as the Fugax silently pops, and all that's left is this sparkling, expanding blue sphere.

Must be weird to be rich.

Not that it was ours to begin with, but just once I'd like to keep one of the things we steal long enough to sell it.

She can't see me rolling my eyes inside my helmet but I do it anyway as I start climbing the grips up to the airlock.

Luz is still laughing when we scramble up into the station and take our helmets off.

"I'm your tight friend," she says. "It's my job to make you do things you don't want to do. When else do you get to have this kind of sin?"

Pretty well never is the answer to that. Life is going to be grim for a while, that's what I'm thinking at this point. Everything I make from my cleaning job goes to pay my dad's indulgence debt and my brother's prison keep, neither of which are shrinking.

If I can't make rent this month, I'll have to beg mercy. Ask the Consilium to put me to work, doing something I don't want to think about. Doing its dirty work on the prison stations, or helping them put people there. It's that or starve to death — or martyrdom as the posters call it. Make myself useful in Heaven since I can't be useful here.

It's different for Luz. She could get denari from her father if she wanted it. But she's always trying to prove that she doesn't want it. Always trying to show that nobody owns her. Like I say, must be weird to be rich.

Luz said she knew a way to get denari and poke the Consilium in the eye. She was right about one thing: that deacon's Fugax was no trouble at all to nab. I thought we were on our way out here to sell it. But she has something else in mind.

The Arcade. I should have known. The only place where we can make really serious denari in a hurry.

You have to go pretty far from the core of the system to find any sin these days. The only Arcade left is in a beaten-up old station right at the fringe of Consilium space, with nothing but void beyond it for as far as you can get.

And now we're here, with no way off since Luz burned the ship. To be fair, it probably had a tracer in it. But also Luz just really likes to blow things up.

The airlock is cramped and smells like my brother's old locker back home. We're the only ones here. Just us and the praesidbots, and they sniff for weapons but don't ask questions. Luz doesn't have any more explosives on her, I guess, or the ones she has don't set off the bots.

"I wish I could see the looks on those deacons' faces when they realize what we did," she says.

"Sure, but they're going to figure out eventually that we ended up here. There's no other station in this direction."

"Eventually, Tamara," she says, patting my shoulder. "Eventually. That's pretty well three games of pinball. Well, three for me. Five for you, brainy."

Heaven help me if she ever figures out I have a Shakespearean scale for her moods. At her best, Luz is Prince Hal, and I'm OK with being Falstaff. At this moment, though, she's gone full Mercutio, which is too bad for me. Being Benvolio is no fun at all.

We're friends, see. We're that kind of friends.

We float in micrograv, getting ourselves ready. Before we go out into the corridor, Luz pulls a hot-pink fabric mask out of a pocket of her suit.

"Did you bring yours?" she asks, her voice muffled as she stretches it over her head, covering her face.

I shake my head.

"I didn't know pinball was in the plan."

We haven't played in months, not since the deacons shut down the Overground. There used to be a whole network of Arcades, back in the slightly better days.

"Plan? No plan," she says, all innocent. "I'm the ball, friend. I goes where I bounce. I just like to be prepared. I've got a condom here"—she pats another pocket—"my last hit of Everlasting here"—another pocket—"and a tampon here."

It's a cute metaphor but there is no ball in pinball. The pins went out after the French Revolution. And the balls went out after the Alignment, but if the Consilium can paint new meanings on shabby old words, then the rest of humanity can too.

"And how much denari do you have?" I ask her.

She shrugs. "640, 650 maybe?"

"Not enough to get us a ride off the station. Enough to send a message to your father, though, to ask him to get us home."

"No way in hell, Tamara. Here."

She pulls out another mask from another pocket, this one plain yellow with splashes of all the colours of the rainbow. My mask.

"Respice finem," Luz says with a grin, making the sign of the pilgrim on her forehead.

I take it. I put it on.

"Well, what's our plan B," I ask, "if the games don't go our way?"

"They will," she says. "If worst comes to worst, we can beg. Who's going to say no to a couple of lost teenaged girls?"

It's unsettling, I have to say, arguing with a grinning hot-pink skull.

"We're not teenagers anymore, Luz."

"We can pass."

With her 640 and my 515, we've got enough for a few launches each, maybe, if we can find someone to take a low bet at first. But this is the Arcade, where everybody's anonymous and nobody can afford to waste their time. It's high stakes just coming here; the deacons raid this place like orrery and the odds of getting assessed for an indulgence are high. Luz's father has been trying to shut the Arcade down, but it's still here. The indulgences must net a lot of denari.

Once I told Luz that her father was one of the good ones in the Consilium. "There are no good ones," she said.

We pass under the big copper sign floating midair in the hallway and suspended by wires that could clothesline you if you're not careful. *Et in Arcadia Ego*, it says. It means, basically, 'I am Everywhere'. By law, it has to be posted in every station, the Consilium's little reminder.

We grab the bars on the walls and pull our way down the hallway, kicking off sideways to float around an unmasked couple who look like virgins and a frat in a spiked teal skinsuit. That frat could be a criminal, could be a deacon sub rosa, or could just be a virgin trying to look tough.

I elbow Luz to tell her *watch out for that sacker*. But we don't see him again.

We arrive at the first group of spheres finally and we put our space helmets and boots in the locker. We have to rent stinky, sweat-stained armour from the bucket, thigh-pads that don't quite fit either of us for different reasons, and thin shoulder pads. We half-joke that we hope we don't take any hard bounces.

Officially there is no gambling at the Arcade, just the fees. We pay the praesidbots to play: 25 denari per game, each. Plus 10 each for the locker rental, and 50 each for the armour, such as it is. Luz has to stick out her tongue to pay and pretty well lick the pay-machine because she keeps her claves in her piercing instead of in her wrist like the rest of humanity.

The Consilium issues us all claves that they can trace, but everybody uses the cloned ones that aren't part of the system. They fool the bots well enough.

"Names?" the bot asks.

"Memento Mori," says Luz.

"Pinxit," I say.

Our high scores come up in lights on the ticker racing around the top of the viewing platform wall. MEMENTO MORI 198,880 PINXIT 130,660.

There's already a frat outside the launchers of one of the spheres, looking for a bet. He's sitting in the air cross-legged. Arrogant sacker had better watch himself or he'll get stuck out of arm's reach of the wall and have to ask someone to give him a push. Big arms and a black mask with smoke tendrils painted on it.

"I'm waiting for someone," he says.

"Then give us the sphere," Luz says. "Or play me while you wait."

He sighs. Luz is so tiny that in her mask, she really could pass for a teenager.

"There's some girls playing in Sphere 7 and they'd probably let you join."

I can feel the words *hey, sacker* coming up my windpipe, and they're out of my mouth before I even think them. Curse words are like vomit sometimes, you know? No way to stop them even though you know it is not going to be pretty.

"Hey, sacker," I say. "This friend is Memento Mori. Check the board."

He glances up at her score, looks down at her, shrugs.

"Easy to rack up points when you're not playing contact."

"I play contact." She's still smiling, by the sound of her voice, or maybe it's just her skull mask playing tricks. "I'll play you for 300."

It's low—the standard is 500. If it were me, I would start even lower, maybe 200, but I'm not Luz. If she loses this, she might not get another chance. Then we'd be even poorer than we started.

The frat sighs like he's just so reluctant, reaches out one arm toward the wall and just barely brushes it with his fingertips. Ha, take your time, sacker, we're not going to help you. He has to wiggle a bit to get purchase and then he pulls himself into the right-hand launcher, throws himself onto the bike.

The spheres are huge and completely transparent. Six plastic bubbles in a circle, each opening onto the viewing platform that encircles them. I can see Luz mount her bike in the left-hand launcher. The bikes in this sphere are small, nimble, one round bumper on the back and one in the front. She pulls herself over to the launch tube on the right, and the frat—he never told us, but he must be BLACKBEARD 145,880—settles into the other, rubbing the bike grips to gear himself up. *Heaven*, I curse under my breath. I've played his kind before.

They both launch fast. Luz hits three bumpers, bang bang bang, racks up 15,000 points before Blackbeard goes into a worm-hole and comes out right at Luz's right flank and bumps her down toward the pit.

This Blackbeard is three times her size and he's playing mean. Not interested in racking up points, he's just trying to send Luz into the big black circle at the bottom of the sphere so it'll be game over and he can take her 300 denari and play someone he thinks is worthy of him.

Luz twists her body and just manages to ricochet off a flipper. Meanwhile the impact with Luz has sent Blackbeard spiralling off toward a tube that slopes a little bit downward. If there were gravity, he'd hit the target at the end, but microgravity is like that, too bad. He goes in but doesn't quite reach the target at the end and has to pull himself out.

Luz is nearly stranded now, all her momentum gone. An object at rest is as good as dead in this game. She's floating in the middle of the sphere. If she can get to a bumper before the frat gets to her, she can start to get some speed up again.

These are smart bumpers, top of the line. They react when an object hits them, and they push it out with greater force than it came in with.

If it were me, I would be avoiding contact with Blackbeard. Not Luz. She hits three bumpers—ring ring ring, flash flash flash—and gets up enough speed, twisting into the last one so it sends her like a bullet at Blackbeard. He slams into the side of the sphere wall so the whole thing shakes.

Ha.

I meet Luz at the exit. A small patch of red blood is seeping through her mask, under her right ear. Helmets aren't allowed anymore, see, because some sacker used one to headbutt another player a while back.

"Easiest 300 I ever made," she whispers, and we fist-bump. I lift the mask and look: it's a small scrape just under the ear, nothing to worry about, but I give that sacker Blackbeard a look anyway. He's wiping off over by the sphere entrance.

"Double or nothing," says Blackbeard, pulling himself over toward us by the wall grips. "Six hundred."

Heaven, those beady eyes would burn holes through his mask if they weren't already there. This frat is looking at Luz like he wants to kill her. And he probably will, if I let her get back into the sphere with him. I'm her tight friend. It's my job to protect her, especially from herself.

Luz is already pulling herself toward her bike, pushing herself from one wall to the other as she goes. She has a way of moving like her whole body's grinning. It's a bad sign when she does that.

I shake my head. "Switch partners. Keep it interesting."

He looks at her, looks at me, looks up at my score.

"Eight hundred," I say. "You play me, it's 800. You play her, it's 600. Oh, you're a big frat, big balls, eh? What's your choice, sacker?"

He shrugs and gestures, a come-here thing with his fingers.

I pull over to Luz, who's lying on her back now in midair, arms crossed, watching me like she's amused.

"Never thought I'd see the day you bet 800," she says. "You really want to do this?"

"I despise this one," I grumble. It's true enough.

If I can beat him, we'll have enough denari to get off this station without having to play any more games. Maybe even a bit left over, more than I had when this day began. The deacons don't know who we are; they only know where we went, or they will soon. If we can get off the station and lie low tonight, we'll be safe.

I kick the bike into the launch tube, my thighs gripping it tight. This is going to be iconic.

Some games, I can feel the endgame stalking me. Once you lose that millisecond of control, each bounce is just good luck or bad luck, and good luck always turns into bad luck sooner or later. That's how it is. Those games, you just have to get it done and try again.

But not this game. Right off the launch I can feel that I've got the advantage this time. That millisecond is on my side; I'm the one stalking the endgame, not the other way around.

I bang the bumpers so hard my ears are ringing, or maybe that's just all the bells going off. Yeah, witness this, Blackbeard, I'm thinking. See what happens when you make Memento Mori's friend Pinxit angry. Tell your friends. I may not have her scores, but I'm bigger than her and I'm smarter than you.

Smack — my face is wet and I breathe in nothing but surface tension. Panic. It's a glob of sweat off Blackbeard. Water in micrograv is bad stuff, like a mask of jelly. I hold my breath until I spin into a tube and then stick out my legs to brace myself and stop long enough to wipe it off. I am so tempted to hit the Tilt button on my bike but I'm up, 34,000 to 27,800, and I don't want to give the sacker the satisfaction.

I pull myself out of the tube and Blackbeard slams into me, taking my breath but giving me momentum. Bumper, target, bonus wheel—I've got it back. Sacker's sweat didn't take me off my game. If Isaac Newton could see me now.

I twirl through a fast tube and I can see him moving toward the tube exit. If I hit him just right, I'll spin him down into the pit, and his 800 will be mine, and we'll be out of here.

Then I just have to breathe in and kick off when I hit the tube exit, to turn my angle just by a hair and speed myself up. I'm coming in fast and I hit him with my front bumper, head on, and down he goes. The sad-trombone sound means I've won.

The impact with Blackbeard sends me spinning up toward the wheels at the top of the sphere. I circle around there for a while, picking up speed off some of the bumpers. I can't remember ever going this fast. As I pass the 50,000 stopper, I lean out far over my bike, gripping the thing with one leg and I smack the stopper.

That's it—new high score for me. 156,000 now, and climbing. My body aches and adrenaline swirls in my brain like the rainbow lights flashing around the sphere. I glance over the entrance and see Luz, watching me, with a half-dozen people behind her. Everybody likes a new high score. Everybody likes to see someone beat the endgame.

I'm not just one millisecond ahead of the endgame now. I'm way out in front. I've only had this feeling a few times in my life, like I'm floating through time and I'm in control. Forget Blackbeard. This is my game and it always was.

This sphere's jackpot is 100,000 denari at 500,000 points. I almost hate to think the thought, but oh heaven, how that denari would save me. I'd pay off dad's indulgence debt, all of it, which he could never do in his own lifetime and I thought I wouldn't be able to do in mine either. I could keep my brother alive in prison. I could pay my own rent and never have to go to the Consilium and wheedle and take a job that hurts people. I could just live my life and breathe. Hard to even imagine what that's like. Must be weird. Seems impossible almost.

The thing about pinball is, once you get up past the likely, the impossible doesn't seem so far.

The sphere shakes and I glance over at the entrance. *Heaven.* A deacon is there, floating like a spectre, holding his prod up.

He's after us because of the stolen Fugax. And he's not even going to wait until the game's up to bring me in.

What does he think he's doing, flying around here with that thing lit up? Deacons are not even supposed to use their prods unless they have to, but I've heard enough stories to know they're all too eager for an excuse. They'd fry us all if they could.

I bang into a corner wicket and slow down, slow way down. When I hit the next bumper, I push against it with my body, getting as much equal and opposite force from it as I can.

Holy of holies, I'm at 496,500.

The emergency door opens. That sacker! The deacon can't power down the sphere, though. These praesidbots are out of the system.

In he floats, with one of his hands holding Luz by the wrist and the other holding his prod. I spit, discreetly, hoping it'll fly the right direction. Two thousand more points is all I need. A few good bumpers, maybe a turn around the wheels.

"By order of the Consilium, you must stop," the deacon whines. It echoes weirdly.

"Laws of physics, friend," I shout. I don't realize how breathless I am until I try to talk. "Object in motion. Stays in motion."

"Tell that sor to come down," he says, shaking Luz. I'm the sor he means.

"You go for the jackpot, you beautiful creature," Luz shouts. She's still wearing her mask, so it's a little muffled. "Never mind this sacker."

At that, the fool deacon pushes off the flipper and comes up toward me. I realize he's trying to engineer a situation, see, where I'll end up on the wrong end of the prod, or Luz will. Or both of us.

And then, just like that, I'm off my game. I lose the lead. The endgame wants me now. It scents my blood. I wipe my face with my arm and look for quick options. If I can get to the 1,000 plunger, that'll do. I'll have to kick my way right past the deacon and Luz, though. Or I can bounce—no, no time. I make my choice and kick.

Too hard.

The deacon sees me coming fast toward him and puts his prod out like he's defending himself. He can't see my face but I can see his, that odious little grin. The penance for hurting or killing a deacon is death, I know that, but I don't have a choice now. I'm in motion.

Luz pushes him away from me and he goes spinning away from her. So it's Luz I run into, hard, and I grab her hand and we spin around each other, like we're dancing. At some point I slip off the bike and it spins over to a bumper, and I swear to everything you believe in that the bike hits and my score goes to 500,005.

So much noise. So much colour.

The deacon is flailing with his prod in one hand and then he just lets go of it, the sacker. I don't know why but he does. I can see it coming straight for us, slow but lit up, and I try to think. No matter how smart you are, there's always going to be a moment when you're not smart enough. If Luz and I just let go we'll float away from each other, but I have no idea whether it'll be fast enough to get us out of the way of that thing. She looks at me and I can tell she's thinking the same.

She'll do anything to get me out of here intact. She's like that. She's always putting herself on the line, like she's taunting death.

We can see the lit-up prod coming for us, our punishment. Probably just a bad burn if it glances off one of us, but maybe worse if it gets enough momentum behind it. Maybe Luz's father has enough denari for the good drugs but even so, they only work sometimes. I can see in the deacon's face that he's thinking death for us would be a providential bounce. Our lives are worth less than nothing.

All the while the jackpot lights are still going off all around and there's a song playing, some horrible tinny thing I've never heard before.

I'm not going to die with the jackpot tune in my head.

I twist my body and push away from Luz, swim desperately in the air even though I know it does no good. One more twist and I grab the prod by the middle, where it's not lit up.

For a second I admit I consider just jamming the end into the deacon, but even I can't outrun a sin sheet with something like that on it. But the thing does come in handy. I use it to bounce off a 50 bumper to my side, change my direction.

The deacon doesn't even see me coming. He's watching Luz. She's hard not to watch, I have to say, her pink skull grinning, her body flailing and rolling.

Bang I go, right into his side, with all my body. It knocks the air out of me. The angle is not exactly what I was going for but it turns out to be perfect. He rolls right into the wormhole, right into the trap where he'll be held for thirty seconds.

Life beats death, sacker, I yell, or maybe I just think it, there inside all that noise and brightness. Life beats death, today, because I say so. Even in the Arcade.

Luz and I bounce our way down into the pit. Probably I could have got a higher score if it weren't for the deacon but I'll take my jackpot and run. My new high score is up on the board now, flashing: PINXIT 501,180.

There will be more deacons coming, and I don't even want to think about the indulgences they'd assess against us now. But they'd have to catch us. They keep playing the game, but they haven't won yet.

Luz and I present our claves, our cloned claves that the Consilium can't trace. We get our denari, then pull ourselves as fast as we can toward the rental bay, and we each jam our claves against the bot (me my wrist, Luz her tongue) to rent one of the old clunkers, nothing like the Fugax but fast enough for our purposes until we can get to the next station. This speedcraft won't be on their list, not yet, not until that deacon reports in. We laugh, because we're still wearing our masks and the rental pads, because we are still alive, because we have a thirty-second lead.

FEATURE INTERVIEW

Kate Heartfield

Pulp Literature: *In my youth, I spent more than a few afternoons at the arcade. Granted, the pinball games were a little different than the one in 'And in the Arcade, Ego'! Could you tell us about the inspiration for this story?*

Kate Heartfield: Sure! It started with my brain one day deciding to pun on the centuries-old phrase *Et in Arcadia ego*, which roughly translates to 'even in a paradise, there I am', with the 'I' being death. That fleeting thought hooked me. I started thinking about the ways that arcade games do have a connection with ego in the modern-psychology sense, with the individual. And with death, at least figuratively speaking. I waited tables in a diner as a teenager, and there was a little arcade attached to it with a pinball machine, a Street Fighter machine, and a few others. After I mopped up, sometimes I'd play a game or two alone in the dark and enjoy the solitude.

PL: *The line, 'You have to go pretty far from the core of the system to find any sin these days' hints at themes of immortality and transcendence — and of survival of the shrewdest. What are your favourite themes to explore?*

KH: I seem to write a lot about women and power, and the relationships between women, and that's true of this story as well. Death definitely comes up a lot! This story is unusual for me in that it explores a kind of theocracy, but what's not unusual for me is the exploration of the role of the individual in political change, and what defiance and compliance can look like.

PL: *Tamara's Shakespearean mood-scale is, forgive the term, next level! Are there any other characters you'd add to the list? May we ask, who are you today?*

KH: Ha! Well, Hamlet is undeniably a mood. Ariel, Lady Macbeth. Most of the characters in *Midsummer*: Puck and Titania for sure, and I've definitely had my Helena moments. These days, I continually feel like Richard II at the moment when he says, "For God's sake, let us sit upon the ground, and tell sad stories of the death of kings."

PL: *Your interactive novels put readers in the centre of the action, and with this story you literally drop your protagonist right into the middle of it all. As an author, do you prefer to write from the midst of things or to gather your insights from the sidelines?*

KH: I find it easiest to build that connection between reader and character by adopting a very close narrative voice. But sometimes, especially as I grow more comfortable with my skills, I enjoy trying more distant approaches and omniscient narrators. One challenge with this story was the contrast between the very tight perspective and the literal vastness of the world that I imply.

PL: *How do you approach world building in your fiction? Other than arcade games, what real-life inspirations have made it into your stories?*

KH: I write in historical settings more often than not (this story's far-future setting is unusual for me), so I draw on real events and real people. For example, my novel *The Embroidered Book*, which comes out in 2022, reimagines the lives of Marie Antoinette and her sister, Maria Carolina of Naples. My first novel, *Armed in Her Fashion*, is now out of print (although it's still in libraries) and was based on real events in Flanders in the fourteenth century, and inspired by medieval and renaissance art and folklore. So I research a lot, and tend to include a lot of detail, always trying for an impression or a suggestion of a greater landscape behind the story.

PL: *As an editor as well as a writer, how do you quiet that analytical voice long enough to get those first drafts down?*

KH: It can be tricky! I am a reviser, and often go through several discrete drafts, especially of book-length work. Paradoxically, that can help me get that first draft down, as I know that nothing is permanent. I tend to use a lot of very simplistic mind-hacks, like twenty-minute sprints with writer buddies (usually online these days). I bought myself an old-fashioned hourglass so that I wouldn't have to use the timer on my phone, and risk getting pulled into notifications. On difficult days, I tell myself to just get three sentences, because that is so obviously achievable. And invariably I write more than three sentences, once I get over myself and get started.

PL: *What authors or titles do you return to over and over again?*

KH: Susanna Clarke's work is just perfect to me and a sheer delight. I read Gregory Maguire, particularly *Wicked*, when I want to recalibrate my writing brain and sense of wonder. Richard Wagamese when I want to remember how to get out of my own way as a writer. Fonda Lee for pure joy and inspiration; she's just such a masterful storyteller. Virginia Woolf to remind myself of where I come from.

PL: *Your latest novel,* The Embroidered Book, *is due out in February 2022. Can you give us a teaser?*

KH: *The Embroidered Book* posits that Marie Antoinette and her sister Maria Carolina discovered a book of magic spells when they were children. It follows them through their adult lives, as they learn how to survive in foreign courts and difficult marriages, and take sides in a secret magical war that mirrors the historical events of the late eighteenth century. It's a big, rich novel that took me several years of hard work, and I'm thrilled to see it out in the world at last. It will be published in February in the UK and a little later in the year in Canada; pre-orders are up already so you can ask your local bookstore!

PL: *Thank you for making the time to speak with us. Before we go, could you tell us a little about what you are working on now?*

KH: I just announced that I'm writing a book set in the Assassin's Creed universe, published by Aconyte Books, which will be out in the summer of 2022. That brings together my prose and gaming lives, and it's a lot of fun and a tremendous privilege. I've also got some other novels in the works, in various states of repair!

Selected Bibliography

Books

The Embroidered Book, 2022 (HarperVoyager UK)

The Magician's Workshop, 2019 (Choice of Games)

The Road to Canterbury, 2018 (Choice of Games)

Alice Payne Rides, 2019 (Tordotcom Publishing)

Alice Payne Arrives, 2018 (Tordotcom Publishing)

Armed in Her Fashion, 2018 (ChiZine Publications)

Short Fiction

'The Course of True Love,' in *Monstrous Little Voices: New Tales from Shakespeare's Fantasy World*, 2016 (Abaddon Books)

PRETTY LIES: EYES FULL OF MOON

Mel Anastasiou

Mel Anastasiou *writes ghost stories and mysteries, including the Fairmount Manor Mysteries, the Monument Studios Mysteries, and the Hertfordshire Pub Mysteries, available at pulpliterature.com. Her novel* Stella Ryman and the Fairmount Manor Mysteries *won a Literary Titan Gold Book Award and was shortlisted for the Stephen Leacock Medal for Humour. 'Eyes Full of Moon' is the next instalment of her forthcoming novel,* Pretty Lies, *an Orpheus tale in a classic British Columbia setting.*

*E*yes Full of Moon

Part 2. In the golden summer of 1974, Jenny Riley is trying to keep herself sane after the crash that killed Joey, the boy next door. She fled to Bowen Island in Howe Sound to see whether the logic and life experience of her older cousin Frances can give her a solid mental footing upon which to move forward in life. But reason and reality bend when the young woman who walked across the surface of the water appears again on the island, and Jenny investigates the increasingly dangerous points of access to a ghost world.

Chapter 4

Howe Sound, Summer 1974

Malcolm Lee dropped his hand, and the green Ford Galaxie sped by with Jenny Riley at the wheel. She didn't wave back, which came as no surprise. He swung the bag of marshmallows at his side, thankful to be young, employed and unloved by any woman.

"That Jenny is worth knowing." Adrian pulled up his yellow shirt and slapped at an insect on his chest. He missed. "Bloody hands *and* a mysterious way about her. I think I'm in love."

"I know where she lives. I saw her house." A skinny kid named Ketchup followed this announcement with kissy noises. Adrian gave him a barbecue chip and he subsided.

"In love? Be my guest." Malcolm kicked a cluster of white everlasting at the side of the road. He and Adrian had been friends since kindergarten, and these days he had to work hard not to hate him. "Anyway, the only thing you love is—"

"Shut up." Adrian shot him a deadly look and then laughed. "Poor Malcolm. Do you want to know what love is, Malcolm? Do you want to know the secret?"

Malcolm looked away. "There is no secret. It's all on TV."

"The secret is that love is all around. Look—over there, love is an alder tree. Male and female in the same plant."

"Tie a can to it," Malcolm said, without hope.

Adrian pointed at a stand of evergreens. "Love is a small brown bird twittering in a tree. Love is pinecones with their dark seed pods no man has ever seen. Look around you, Malcolm, because here are the most beautiful fruits of love—these horrible children in yellow shirts. That's what love produces."

Malcolm snatched up an alder branch from the side of the road and snapped off the twigs, then cursed as someone stepped on the heel of his shoe. He turned to find Ketchup at his back. Ketchup wrestled the stick away from him and ran off, whacking the salmonberry bushes.

"Get off the road," Malcolm shouted. Ketchup stuck out his thumb at a pickup. It rolled by him.

"You can't protect them," Adrian said. "It's impossible."

"It's literally our job, Adrian."

"Then we're earning money for nothing. What a happy thought. To celebrate, I'm going into the woods for a pee."

"I'm coming too," Ketchup called, waving his stick and nearly taking out the eye of the kid on his right.

Adrian said over his shoulder, "No, you'll pee out your cabin window the way God intended."

Malcolm watched him go. He switched the bag of marshmallows to the hand furthest from the kids and jerked the stick away from Ketchup. He threw it towards the trail Adrian had taken into the woods.

Adrian wasn't going for a pee. *You can't protect them.*

He pushed the thought away. Instead he considered his encounters with Jenny Riley, yesterday on the ferry and today in the store. He thought about her grey eyes, warm when they looked at you, sad when they looked away, and how the wind had caught her long brown hair as she'd stood on the ferry deck and gazed out to sea.

Chapter 5

Jenny walked out to the front porch through the gap where Frances's living room sliding glass door used to be. Beyond Corner Bay, the noon ferry to the Sunshine Coast hummed across the Sound.

Frances sat with her feet up on the railing and a cloth-backed tome splayed across her lap. She held a thick builder's pencil and slashed a large cross over a page of the book. "That bloody man Gig Chalmers. Does it seem odd to you that the most successful people in the most demanding fields are supreme only in their self-confidence?"

"I guess jerks are all around us. Including me. I'm sorry."

"Oh, yes, I already swept up all the glass you broke." Frances turned a page over and made a great tick in the margin. "Don't worry about the sliding door. Or don't worry about it *much.*"

"Sorry. And for borrowing your car."

"Borrowing it?"

"Yes."

Frances smiled down at her book. "Did you really borrow it or did you actually steal it and bring it back?"

"Borrowed it."

"And?"

"I could use some more advice."

"Gosh. Well, in my opinion, you shouldn't break any more sliding glass doors. What do you think of my missing door, by the way? On the good side, I'll never have to wash it. And on rainy days I can splash barefoot through puddles in the living room. On the bad side, deer can walk right into the living room and roam around the kitchen."

"I'll keep apologizing until you tell me to stop."

"Stop."

"Thanks." Jenny looked down at the book on Frances's lap at the photograph of a mosaic leopard. "But what should I do to get over this ..." She was stymied for the right word, because after months of counselling, the words *grief* and *sorrow* had taken on a professional-use-only vibe, as if you needed a doctorate to say them out loud. "... this heartbreak?"

"Work. That's how you'll move onwards." Frances slapped the open page of her book and leaned forward, as if sensing her moment. "This is a brilliant mosaic, wherein Orpheus strides singing into Hades to bring back his dead true love."

"Eurydice."

"*Gesundheit.* No, seriously, you're right. Her name was indeed Eurydice, and the fact that you know it is more evidence that you should be pursuing a career in archaeological studies."

"You might be exaggerating, Frances."

"Not at all. But I don't want to convince you. I would rather show you, on the actual mosaic in the UK. Because if I don't get to the dig before Gig Chalmers, he will pluck the Orpheus mosaic out of the ground and slap it on the wall of the British Museum with a sign reading *All my own work.* I already named you in my prospectus as my assistant. Are your marks good? Don't answer, I looked them up with the registrar."

"But what if I go with you to England and I get worse? You'd have to practically parent me, and at my age."

"No, at *my* age." Frances frowned. "All right, you have a point. Improve, and then work. But you're going to have to put some welly into it. A week's deadline to buy charter flight tickets to the UK. I can hold Chalmers off for a few days yet. So, in the meantime, work on improving yourself."

"How?"

"Read *I'm Okay, You're Okay.*"

"But that posits that I'm okay."

"Jokes about your state of misery seem a positive sign. Maybe your next step is to associate with people who are not, like your unlucky true love, passed on from this world. My reading suggests that some people find socializing with living, breathing friends is an antidote to grief, depending on the friends."

"What friends? I don't know anybody on Bowen except you."

"Well, I'm nicely alive, so I count. Also, somebody who at least knows you left a note in our mailbox." Frances pulled a folded slip of paper out from under her sketch and passed it to Jenny.

A breath of wind plucked the folded paper from between Jenny's fingers and tossed it away over the rocks. There it drifted down onto the water and sank.

Jenny almost laughed aloud. "I call that a dead end. Should I try the Primal Scream again?"

"*No.*"

"Frances, I need one of your psychological ideas."

"You flushed all my ideas down the toilet of your non-cooperation and then broke my sliding glass door. I have nothing more to offer."

"No other therapies? I can't believe it."

France's face lit up. "There were historical treatments. For example, they used to take crazy people and throw them in with snakes, because they thought that terror that would make a sane person crazy, and would work reflexively to make a crazy person sane."

Bowen Island was rich in sometimes startling but always harmless garter snakes. "But I'm not afraid of snakes. Except for poisonous ones."

"Well, they also used electric shock." Frances stretched her sandaled feet out in front of her and wiggled her toes. Her book slid off her knee and thudded to the floor.

"Lord. Anything else?"

"One other thing. They'd tie crazy people into cold baths. I suppose it was meant as a shock to the unsettled mind. Or maybe the cold calmed the nervous folks and cooled down the hotheads."

"Which am I?"

"Some of each, I'd say."

Of course, Frances's little house on the water had no bathtub, and Jenny doubted that a shower would serve. Or, no. How stupid. Of course the house had a bath. Corner Bay right here in front of her would be cold in summer and death in winter. The bay was a bath as big as all outdoors.

It was July. The sun was hot. Never was there a better time to test out an antique theory for improving one's mental health. Jenny bent, picked up Frances's book with both hands, and handed it back to her. She ran down the stairs, past Frances's old rowboat, and over the rocky shore to the rock and barnacle beach. You left your shoes on to swim in Frances's bay, and Jenny teetered at the water's edge, the toes of her runners almost but not quite wet. She had long ago developed a method for entering cold water. She would pretend to be someone she detested, and then she would send that person into the water. In the primary grades she'd pretended she was Belle, the line budger. Now she was grown-up, she used Joey's buddy Lerner, the one with the smelly waxed canvas coat. She'd freeze Lerner north to south any day. Of all Joey's so-called friends, she hated Lerner most.

Jenny stepped into the water. It was chilly enough to make an impression on anybody, no matter their mental state. She looked over her shoulder at the porch rail where Frances leaned on her elbows, watching. No matter what Frances's research had found out about craziness, Jenny would bet her small savings account that she could not be made any saner or less loss-assaulted by submerging herself in cold water. She imagined herself, one in a line of crazy people, in her own long tin tub with a canvas cover pulled tight across the top and just her head poking out. Hair haywire, eyes closed and rolling under their lids. Lines of tubs down a white-tiled room with no windows, no soap or hot water. Never getting clean, never getting sane, only colder and colder, like a dead person. Like Joey.

Still, Jenny owed Frances a good effort at least, to make up for the broken door. She splashed into the bay, up to her hips, where the water seeped upwards from the hem of her shirt. Now she was up to her neck. Her hair fanned out along the surface of the water.

She went under smoothly, as if a hand were helping her down. As if somebody already under the water wanted company and had reached up to pull her down. *Shh.* The whole point of this exercise was to shut out crazy thoughts.

And, despite the cold, it was peaceful under the surface of the water. It felt smooth against her arms, her face, even her stomach where her shirt billowed out in the water. She could understand how the crazy people tied into tin tubs responded to the water's calming effect, too, although they didn't get to duck their heads. She supposed there would have been danger of drowning. But she wouldn't drown. Not Jenny. She waved her arms about to keep herself underwater. She was not quite out of her depth here, and rocks rolled beneath the soles of her running shoes. Her forearm brushed something slick — seaweed, maybe. She opened her eyes in the mottled light a few inches below the surface of the bay. At first all she could see was her own hair, turned from brown to red-gold by the diffused light around her. Her fingers had hooked a strand of seaweed, and she brushed it away from her face.

Look again.

A green hair ribbon hung tangled in the seaweed. Jenny spiralled underwater and looked into a pair of pale eyes set in a woman's face and suspended in the water.

She has pearls for eyes.

Jenny gasped and took a mouthful of cold salt water up her nose and down her throat. She struck out with her feet, to push herself backwards and away from Moira. Her knee hit bottom and she kicked hard but didn't rise.

Strong hands took Jenny by the shoulders and held her down. Jenny struggled, but Moira's grip was steady.

Pretty.

Jenny read Moira's lips. *Pretty, but not as pretty as me.*

Jenny kicked again against the slick rocks at the bottom of the bay. Her struggle only agitated bubbles that blinded her to everything but their own bright light and chaos of movement. She lost all sense of up and down.

Just when she was certain she was done, she felt a tug at her shirt collar. Somebody yanked her upwards. Jenny got one foot under her and thrust against rocks and mud. Her head broke the water. She stood on shaking legs, hip-deep, coughing, and then sat down hard in the shallows.

Frances gave a gasping breath and let go of Jenny's shirt collar. "Please tell me this is as difficult as you get."

Jenny whispered, "I need to say that I scraped a dent into the Galaxie's fender."

"Of course you did." Frances lay flat in the shallow water, her hair spread out in wet ropes. "I bet I look like Ophelia's mother, if floating ran in the family."

Jenny's nose was running, and she wiped a smearing fist across her face. She crawled out of the water atop the black rocks on shore. Overhead seagulls flew and cried.

Frances asked, "What if we try a new tack? Forget the crazy cures for insanity. If you want to be normal then do ...? Finish the sentence."

"... do normal things. Like what?"

"What's normal for you isn't normal for me. What if you

select some activity that is inspired and supported not by your wild imagination — or mine — but by practicality and your own generationally normative needs? Me, I'm going to take a hot shower."

She headed back to her house. Jenny followed and showered quickly in the guest bathroom, changed into dry clothes, and hung her wet things out on the deck railing.

What could she do that was normal for her? It was past noon. Jenny slipped into the kitchen and opened all the cupboards. Behind a dusty jumble of pans she found a large yellow bowl. When she hauled it out, a dead mouse slid across the bottom, brown and dry as a leaf. She took the bowl into the backyard and tipped the corpse into a clump of ferns. Then she soaped and rinsed the bowl five times and set it on the kitchen counter. The bowl was yellow on the outside and white inside, like an egg turned inside out in the fourth dimension. You could cook out of this bowl your whole life. You could use it every day for eighty years, die in your bed, and this bowl would be sitting on the counter, as round and golden as ever, when they carried you out past it.

She set it on the counter. Frances was apparently still bathing, so Jenny drove the Galaxie back to the general store, made a few purchases, and returned with them moments before Frances emerged from her room with her hair still wet.

"No more Ophelia death drama, please."

"Got it. Listen, about Hamlet. He was busy investigating his father's death, but I always wondered: did Ophelia drown herself, or was she pushed?"

"Public opinion says she waded into the water, broken-hearted and dragging her dresses."

"But doesn't Shakespeare write, *Men have died from time to time, and worms have eaten them, but not for love?*"

Not for love. Naught for love. Tied in knots for love.

Frances said, "Give me a cup of tea and stop quoting at me. I'm trying to remember what that note from your friend said."

Jenny made her a cup of tea. "Frances, I need something from you."

"Shh. Was there something in the note about the colour orange? Or green. I swear, since you came to visit and started breaking things, I'm losing my mind."

Jenny pulled flour, yeast, and olive oil out of a grocery sack and set them on the counter next to the yellow bowl. "I have to tell you something. I warn you, though, you'll think I'm crazy."

"Don't worry about that." Frances folded her hands under her chin. "I already think you're crazy."

"And I don't expect you to believe me."

"Just go ahead and tell me, difficult one."

"First, I'm not crazy."

"Yes, you are. Everybody's crazy. Normalcy is a sliding scale, and the way the world is unfolding, somebody should adjust the bell curve every year—"

"Frances …"

"To be honest, after all the reading I've done, I don't think your problems are about crazy or normal, I think they're all about obvious or hidden—"

Jenny held her hands against the side of her head. "Are you finished?"

"I hope not, though I suppose a woman in her fifties must seem old to you."

"Frances …"

"I was just trying to make you laugh. But go on, keep talking about yourself, and remember that I can cope with oppositions like irrationality in a sane young woman such as yourself."

"Right. *Now* are you finished?"

"Yes."

Jenny took a deep breath. "Do you believe in ghosts?"

"No."

With a blast of clarity not unlike what people must feel having their sinuses cleaned out with a rubber hose, Jenny's head cleared. She opened a packet of fast-rise yeast and swished a spoonful around in the flour. In a saucepan she mixed up oil and warm water and splashed a little on her wrist.

"What's that for?" Frances leaned over the countertop.

"Yeast has got to be baby-bottle temperature. Too hot and it dies."

Frances said, "All right. I admit I do."

"Do what?"

"I believe in ghosts."

"You do not. You just said you didn't." Jenny stirred the warm liquids into the dry ingredients and powdered the counter with flour.

"I do, actually."

"I heard that *actually* is a word people use when they're lying."

"But I'm not lying. I believe that ghosts are everywhere."

Jenny was surprised to see a tear fall from her eyes into the dough. But it was only salt water and no harm done. She turned the sticky mess out onto it to the counter to knead.

Frances said, "Do you have to cry when I agree with you? That's very Ophelia indeed."

"I'm nothing like her, stop worrying. Do you really believe in ghosts?"

"Sort of. I believe that we've all got ghosts. These ghosts are secrets, guilt, and memories we don't want to recall. Genetics and upbringing are both ghosts. Moments when we wish we'd stood up and spoken out. Moments when we wish we'd sat down and shut up."

"You're just using ghosts as metaphors for *baggage*. Like a grief counsellor." Jenny turned the dough over and slapped it down hard on the counter.

"But at least you've stopped crying. Now, you must admit that ghosts shouldn't look like people, because seagulls would make much better receptacles for dead human souls." Frances waved a hand at the calling gulls circling Corner Bay. "Look at those birds, white against the blue sky, crying out like Persephone, *It's not so bad here*, while they peer down at us from the heavens with their bright black eyes, hoping for a crust of bread, something from the world of men to which they don't belong."

Jenny pounded and folded the dough. It felt warm, alive under her fist. "I'm talking about genuine ghosts. Traditional dead spirits. Can you, just for one moment, suspend your disbelief?"

Frances sighed. "I will hang it high."

"If you were haunted by actual ghosts . . ."

"Not metaphors? Not seagulls?"

"If you saw the ghost of a dead person and heard her speak to you, would you answer?" She slapped the dough back into the big yellow bowl and laid the clean tea towel over the top. "What would you do?"

"Maybe nothing. Maybe these spirits would be part of the natural surroundings, like trees — like spiders, popping out of places and startling people, but essentially just doing their own thing. *I've got ghosts*, you could say, like you'd say *I've got mice*."

But mice didn't whisper in your ear. Or place hands on the top of your head and push you underwater.

Frances went on, "Alternatively, you might consider the psychology of the individual."

"My father says that." Jenny remembered the sound of the chainsaw as he cut through the garage wall to haul her out of the stored wrecked yellow Zed. Had her father imagined she'd turn on the motor with the doors shut? "He says some people have a harder time getting over things than others."

"Sure. But I meant the psychology of the individual haunting you."

Jenny peered at her cousin, but Frances's long hair was screening her face and she could read nothing.

She said, "This ghost is always in the water. That, or she's on it."

"She? How strange. I was sure you were talking about a male ghost."

No. Yes. Jenny held one shaking hand with the other.

Frances said, "Spaghetti and garlic bread."

"What?"

"The letter. I've got it. I retrieved it in my head. It read something like, *To Jenny. There's spaghetti and garlic bread tonight. You haven't lived until you've seen one hundred kids in one place eating spaghetti. Six o'clock, stay for campfire. Signed, some fellow.*"

"Adrian. Or Malcolm. They work at the summer camp." The camper with the stick must have told them where she lived.

Frances snapped her fingers. "There was a *PS*. It said, *For dessert, there's yellow Jell-O.*"

Jenny frowned. She could go to the camp and eat spaghetti. Alternatively, and more attractively, she could simply go to bed and sleep. But she couldn't go to bed forever. Although some people did. Depressed people, dying people, crazy people, went to bed and never came back.

She said lightly, "I hardly know Adrian and Malcolm. I'll stay home instead, and keep you company. We can eat this bread hot from the oven."

"Ha. I knew you'd find a way to refuse the society of your peers, stay in with me. Yes, stay with me, your middle-aged aunt, and may the sins and virtues of our respective self-destructive fathers and boyfriends not be invested in us, the survivors."

"Very funny."

"No, not funny. Insightful. Literary, even, since I've offered you the exact opposite of the theme of Ibsen's *Ghosts*. If you do stay home, do you want to read the play out loud tonight? *Ghosts*? I've got a copy on my bookshelf. It's even grimmer than you."

By the time the sun slanted at a late afternoon angle, Jenny had pulled the loaf of bread out of the oven and presented it to Frances to have with her supper. Outside on the beach, she pulled Frances's rowboat down the algae-slick boards that served as a slip and pushed off out of Corner Bay towards the summer camp where Malcolm and Adrian worked. She turned to face east and rowed west, lining up a tree on the far side of the bay with the centre of the stern to keep her wake straight.

She stroked hard, shoving the waves back. She passed Winona Bay, next to Corner, where wood-framed homes emitted smells of coffee and hot briquettes. She rowed on past acres of Crown land, where cedars seemed to grow straight up out of the Sound. She kept her course and never looked down into the water.

CHAPTER 6

Malcolm kicked at a burnt log beside the camp fire pit. Ashes covered his shoe. Adrian stood above him on a weathered cedar bench, where after supper the campers would sit at campfire.

Malcolm said, "Your kids threw all my kids' sleeping bags into the bushes. You have to make them get the bags back."

"Sure thing, pal. I'll do that, and then I'll spin straw into gold. By the way, I'm winning."

Malcolm shook his head. "I already won — she's coming to dinner."

"Oh, was that the bet?"

"Sure thing, pal."

"That shows," Adrian said, "how little you know."

Malcolm rubbed at the blackened rubber tread on his runners and watched his friend amble off towards the camp's front gate. He instructed himself to stop wondering whether Jenny would accept his invitation to dinner, and, if so, whether she would arrive by land or sea. If by sea, Malcolm would see her first. If by land, Jenny would find Adrian waiting for her at the arched driftwood gate, all set to charm her socks off.

Malcolm shoved his hands into his pockets and abandoned all hope. He did so while gazing out across Howe Sound towards Gambier Island and was therefore perfectly located to see Jenny rowing towards camp. She turned and raised her hand to him. He waved back.

"I don't need this," he muttered to himself. Still, here he was, standing on the seashore with sand in his shoes, engaged in a romantic competition he didn't want to enter. Against Adrian, who always won.

Malcolm walked down to the water's edge. Jenny rowed closer. She was a strong oarswoman, he judged, although possibly he was such a fool that he'd judge anything she did as well done. But she kept a straight wake and made a silent passage, whereas he'd have been catching crabs and complaining.

The rowboat butted against the sand, and he took hold of the gunwale. Jenny climbed out, and the two of them hauled the dinghy a couple of lengths above the tide line beside a rack of canoes and orange lifejackets.

She bent down and ran her hands through the mottled grey sand. "Lucky. Frances's beach only has barnacles and rocks."

"They carted this sand in by boatloads in the thirties. Every summer, we lose a little."

"Erosion?"

"The director says it goes home in the kids' shoes."

Jenny laughed, but he hadn't meant to be funny. She slapped sand off her palms and peered into the trees above the beach, as if she were looking for somebody.

Malcolm said, "I'll show you around camp."

He led her through the cedars lining the beach to the cookhouse, with its tin roof that sounded a danceable beat when it rained. A few of the cookhouse workers were slinging plates and ketchup bottles onto the picnic tables in the dining porch. They angled past the pass-through serving window to the kitchen, which smelled of tomatoes and burnt spaghetti.

"My kids are at the cabin, getting ready for supper," Malcolm said. "At least they are in some ideal parallel world."

Jenny peered at the camp gate. "You must get good sunsets."

"Sure, on the beach at campfire. That'll be after supper. I've already laid the fire."

"You do work hard. What about Adrian over by the gate, lying on the bench? Shouldn't he be looking after kids or something?"

Malcolm trudged after Jenny towards the lone, romantic figure stretched out on the bench where the cookhouse gang took their smoke breaks.

Adrian opened one eye. "Jenny. How did I miss your advent? Did you rise from the sea in an oyster shell? Did you stroll along the beach with the wind in your hair and a rented dog, like sad old Richard Nixon?"

"Whatever you'd like to think, surfer boy," Jen returned.

"I think I do like to think." Adrian sat up.

Malcolm, Jenny, and Adrian navigated a salal-covered knoll to two small green-roofed cabins, one old and one ancient. Since it was just before supper, there ought to have been a lot of small boys washing up at the black rubber hose hung over the trough next to the cabins, but the area was empty. A scuffling sound led them to a stand of bushes between the cabins. There they found a clutch of unwashed campers picking and eating huckleberries.

"Wash yourselves, please." Malcolm caught sight of the thin grey neck on Flash, the kid nearest him. All his kids were as dirty as a mechanic's thumb. Still, none of them had come down sick with anything yet, at least not anything that he'd had to wipe up. "Time to eat."

"We did wash, but the dirt won't come off." Flash was still wearing yesterday's T-shirt, and only the ghosts of his ancestors knew how long he'd been wearing his underwear.

"That's Roy and Tony over there with the dirty pants," Adrian told Jenny. "Anik's got the snotty nose. Those are Ketchup,

Tanaka and Flash. I don't know where the rest are. Maybe spitting out of windows."

"Search for the great *Freakies* tree," Ketchup intoned. "There you will find answers."

"Come on, people," Malcolm called, and for once they came. "Sorry, usually I'm no damn good at this."

"Show-off." Adrian glanced sideways at Jenny, who laughed. He led the group towards the dining porch, and Malcolm kicked small branches off the trail. Behind the adults, the little boys talked full steam about their day, truth and fiction, the same baloney every night. Only the details varied—prickle bushes along the trails, squirrels in the branches, and great white sharks off the swimming beach waiting to skin their young bones. The chatter rose as they ran ahead to the covered dining porch, where the whole group stopped dead.

A dozen tables lay on the ground, legs pointing upwards. Serving bowls of spaghetti in tomato sauce were set in front of them on the plank floor.

"Prank?" Malcolm asked.

Adrian shrugged.

"Somebody must be mad at you guys," Tanaka said.

"Why should anybody be?" Jenny asked.

"Only the *Freakies* tree knows." Tanaka poked his finger into the bowl of spaghetti. He picked up a handful of noodles and slapped it against Ketchup's yellow shirt.

Malcolm said to Jenny, "Sorry about that. You're a long way from civilization."

Jenny's look was unreadable. Everything she did was damned unreadable. The trick was not to care.

"**Give up on the bet yet?**" Adrian scraped the last of the dishes into the washtub and flicked tomato sauce across the fly of Malcolm's shorts. Malcolm dipped his hand in a half-empty bowl of sauce and drew a wet red cross over Adrian's heart.

"She's a person, Adrian. She might even be a friend. I don't bet on friends."

"The best thing about you, Malcolm, is that you always see everyone opposite to what they are."

"You don't think she's a friend?"

"A blind man could see that she doesn't care about this evening, or you. Not even me, much. Yet."

"I don't know why I even talk to you."

Adrian nodded. "Listen, she might be my dream girl."

Malcolm couldn't think of an answer that wouldn't raise the stakes, so he said nothing and flung cutlery into the washing pan.

When the summer darkness fell, and the children trailed away to the hissing orange campfire, Jenny stood between the two of them and asked, "Can one of you help me down with my boat?"

Malcolm stepped in front of Adrian to block. "One of us can."

"Thank you. Can I ask you a question?" She looked from Malcolm to Adrian. "If you lost something that you really cared about, what would you do?"

"Do without."

"Get it back."

Malcolm said one or the other. He was paying too little attention to his own words and too much to the line of her cheek in the setting sun.

Jenny pulled her oars out from under the dinghy seats. She wore such a serious expression that he desired to make her laugh again. But Malcolm could only ever remember one real joke, and this didn't seem the moment to tell it. He wished to god Jenny were plain, or that he were handsome.

Back off.

He started. It was almost as if someone had whispered in his ear. But Adrian was already disappearing among the trees, and Jenny was hauling the dinghy along the sand by its painter rope. Malcolm hurried to help.

Back the hell off.

Chapter 7

Night fell. Jenny rowed away from the camp towards Frances's bay. She kept the black lacework of trees to her left and the flat evening waters of Howe Sound to her right. A swallow, or maybe a bat, flicked past her head down to the water and swooped towards shore. If Joey were here, he would have stretched out in the bottom of the rowboat and gazed up at the stars. He would have counted the stars in a sports announcer's voice, or thought up ridiculous pet names for them. Or he would have curled up and gone to sleep, like Adrian tonight on the bench back at camp.

A wave slapped the bottom of the rowboat, sending it rocking. Jenny lifted her oars out of the water and rocked with the boat while the second wave hit, and the third. Ferryboat waves felt like this, but the ferry had long passed by. Two more rolling waves lifted and dropped her. Above the rattle of wooden oars on metal oarlocks she thought she heard a voice, but she couldn't work out what it said, or where it came from.

Another wave hit—the last, for now. The water around the boat drew out flat again. And then, directly into her ear, like warm breath on a cool evening, she heard Joey's voice.

Together forever. Get into the car.

Here it was: even out here on the water, sorrow sniffed after her like a dog and spoke in Joey's voice. Tears filled the corners of her eyes. She rowed harder still. She was in mourning, and that thought ought to help her keep her perspective—or, if her own was too battered and unreliable, then somebody else's perspective. For example, what would Frances say about hearing Joey speak? Frances might say that on such a quiet night, voices travelled uncannily well, and someone a hundred paces away might sound as if he were standing next to you. Someone could be standing among the Crown land trees for whatever reason, talking to her in a voice like Joey's.

Jenny pulled at the oars. It felt as if something were pulling back. Under her feet, where the soles of her running shoes touched the thin wooden bottom of the boat, she could feel movement. A sort of swift, shifting rush. The unseen movement grew stronger, as if all the fish near Corner Bay—no, all the fish in the Sound, blennies and bullheads, flatfish, shiners, and bass—had come out for a night swim under her rowboat. Jenny let go the oars and held onto the gunwales.

A shape rose swiftly out of the water, as if the figure were running up a set of stairs. Without a splash or a by-your-leave, Moira grasped the stern corners of the rowboat, looped one leg and then the other over the transom, and slid herself down to sit on the stern plank seat. She kept her knees together modestly and tucked her feet, neat in strappy shoes, underneath. Her dress and hair were quite dry.

"The wind keeps untying my ribbons. I've lost one of them already." Moira leaned over the side of the boat and peered into the dark water, which showed no reflection.

Jenny pulled her feet as far back as possible under her seat in the centre of the rowboat. She knocked one of the oars loose and caught it before it could drop into the water.

"I think I'm late," Moira said. "Or maybe Philip's behind time again. What time is it?"

Jenny held still. "I don't know. Past ten thirty, I think."

"Philip can tell time by the stars." The air was warm around them.

"Can he?"

"He says he can. Look at that sky, velvet and diamonds. Doesn't it make you feel rich and romantic? The last time I saw Philip, he scooped me into his arms like I was a goddess fallen to earth and he'd caught me before I hit ground. But he seems to have cooled off some." Moira's shoe brushed Jenny's foot.

Jenny pushed her feet back further under her seat.

"In fact, he seems to have cooled off a lot," Moira said. "Ye gods and little fishes, it's so hard to keep a man. The lies you have to tell. Let's get down to brass tacks, shall we? I need you to come with me."

"Where?" Jenny glanced at the water and held her oars tighter.

"Shipboard party. I'll make him take a break in his duties and dance with me, and then you dance with him and give him the full treatment for me. For example, we might try to make him jealous, and you could say *A handsome fellow took Moira to a show*. Would that make Philip sit up and take notice? Perhaps. But one time I bought myself a box of chocolate cherries and wrote a note that read, *To Moira, sweet as candy*. And did it work?"

Jenny shook her head.

"Right you are, sister. Philip ate half the box and never asked where it came from. I'm tired of playing these games alone." From somewhere in her skirts, Moira produced a small flat bottle. "Gin?"

"No. Thanks."

"You're not very prudent, are you? Drinking before a dance saves money."

Jenny swallowed her laugh. "My boyfriend always said much the same."

"Jenny with the long brown hair, let's talk about your fellow. Because fair's fair." Moira took a sip from her bottle. "You have a boyfriend, but you talk to other fellows on the beach at night."

"I don't."

"Talk to other fellows?"

"Have a boyfriend. He —"

"Don't give up hope, sister. I'm here to help." Moira took a drink from her bottle. "Do you think I should play hard to get or go after Philip? Should I be easy and uncomplicated, or difficult and worth the hunt?"

Jenny said, "I don't know."

"You do know. My heart is breaking, Jenny. I need a friend to help me wage a little war on love. You're my comrade at arms, my friend to tell Philip some pretty lies. I'm your friend, and I'll help you get your own fellow back. Now, let's go and make a stunning entrance at this party. We'll be the two prettiest girls on the boat."

Moira stood, stepped out of the rowboat, and left it rocking under Jenny. She walked a few steps away across the water, stopped, and held out her hand.

"Come along, now. Don't you want to get our true loves back from wherever their hearts might wander?"

Jenny said, "Wait." She shipped the oars, stood up, and leapt out of the boat after Moira.

A second later she was alone again, flailing about in the waters of the Sound. She smacked her head against the side of the boat, gasped, and sucked in a mouthful of water. She clawed hold of the bow and raised herself up on her elbows in hopes of heaving herself into the little boat, but she couldn't muster the strength. She lost a running shoe and imagined following the shoe downwards, her hair curling round her, reaching out for the shoe while stars stirred above on the surface of the water. Maybe Moira would return and find her down there, a pale figure in the dark water, refracted moon rays striking lights in her hair. The thought almost caused her to lose her grip on the dinghy's bow.

She kicked off her other running shoe and let it drop to follow its mate. Movement became easier, and she pulled herself hand over hand around the side of the boat to the stern. There she found purchase for one bare heel on the gunwale. Mustering strength and sinew, she levered herself back inside the boat, took hold of her oars, and set off alongside the rocky shores for Centre Bay.

§

If there's a ghost, is there a ghost world? And if Orpheus nearly saved Eurydice, what are Jenny's chances of getting Joey back from the other side? Issue 34's instalment takes us deeper and deeper still into the mystery of *Pretty Lies.*

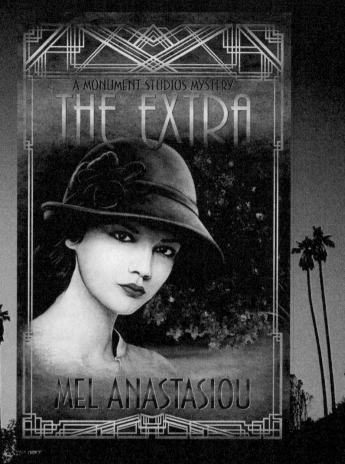

A MONUMENT STUDIOS MYSTERY

THE EXTRA

MEL ANASTASIOU

The casting call is murder

VESSEL

Cara Waterfall

*Ottawa-born and Costa Rica–based, **Cara Waterfall** has poetry in*
Best Canadian Poetry, The Fiddlehead, The Night Heron
Barks, *and more. She won* Room's *2018 Short Forms contest,*
Room's *2020 Poetry Contest, and the Editors' Choice Award for*
Pulp Literature's *2020 Magpie Award for Poetry. In 2019,*
she was a finalist for Radar Poetry's *Coniston Prize and a*
shortlisted candidate for the CBC Poetry Prize. She has a diploma
in Poetry and Lyric Discourse from The Writer's Studio at SFU.
Visit her at carawaterfall.com.

$\mathcal{V}$ESSEL

His words enact laws
upon your body that unlight

the speech within you. You would do
anything to escape the glare.

What is a spotlight on a body,
but a subject uncomfortably lit?

A bullseye for the coming arrow?

I imagine the moment he pelts slurs
upon you, how you shrivel

as each diatribe arrives like a detonation's
wave, pounding you flat,

how you swallow the weight
of a pause after he pinches your arm

and the whole room tilts — until
you hand him the knife that cuts

your heart out.

§

The tightrope between school and home
is one continuous warp.

The entry wound of a slur has no exit —
it simply remolds itself into self-loathing.

In your face, I read the day: mornings being led
to slaughter, harrowing hallway walks,

glances that make you flinch as if slapped.
What will raise his hackles next?

Nightly, I learn the tendency of bodies
to remain where they fall.

Not even sleep's fortress is safe.
Your sadness germinates in darkness.

I gather you in my arms and try
to put you back together. I know

you want love to crawl back in,
but there's no room left.

Vessel

§

Son, what shall I do? Shall I collapse
the narrow back of public decorum?

Force him to hear a child's agonizing silence,
its weight bearing down like the mass

of some ill-fated asteroid?

Or shall I prostrate him upon
the altar wild, abandon all reason

& let the carnage be mine?

O, my little ghost muted,
what you feel is one thing;

what you don't say: another.

§

The heart's soft lattice disappoints
again, contracts around the pain,

like a palm around a splinter—as if
attempting to squeeze a balm.

But the fox does not scream
without cause.

Who can know the burden of living
in the dark, fingertips fanning

across every face he's reading
trying to understand love?

PAPER, CANDLES, HEARTS, AND OTHER COMBUSTIBLE MATERIALS

Anne Baldo

Anne Baldo's *first collection of short fiction is forthcoming from* Porcupine's Quill. *Anne's previously published fiction appears in* Hermine, Carousel, Into the Void, *and* subTerrain.

Paper, Candles, Hearts, and Other Combustible Materials

When Franco sees the front page of the paper, he thinks of course Jules would wear something like that to burn a place down. Yellow hoodie, a snake on the back, blood-red roses on the sleeves. It is Jules for sure in the photograph taken from surveillance footage, even with its gritty quality, murky like the tabloid snaps people used to claim were the Loch Ness monster, or Elvis eating pancakes in a roadside diner. Jules, under the headline *OPP Releases Image of Suspect in Restaurant Fire*. Franco doesn't have to pick up the phone, make the call — *If anyone has information please contact* — but he will. He does. He wants to be the one.

Cedar can't sleep. The hotel room is so cold it hurts. Franco over dinner earlier, at the casino's steakhouse, knife half-sunk in a slab of charred octopus, a thorny salad on the side, saying *Maybe you need to see a doctor*. But Cedar had. The doctor and his clean, even nails, medicinal cologne: — bloodroot and crushed aspirin — flicking a prescription slip, his eyes never leaving the screen of the laptop as he quickly clicked the keys. A bottle of pills, *take twice daily for nerves*. She swallowed them for a week, and hated them: the way they muddled her, left her sluggish and damp. So stunned she couldn't catch her own thoughts long enough to dwell on anything. They lumbered slowly on, drowsy sheep, but just ahead of her always, leaving her mind a flat, empty field. A void is not peace. Nothingness is not the same as happiness. She threw the pills out. *Because you always want the quick fix*, Franco says.

At the steakhouse, Cedar orders macaroni and cheese.

You could try the baked escargot—

It's like chewing on someone's used gum, Cedar says. Franco shrugs into his rye.

Now Franco is asleep in their hotel room, television on. The blue light flickers over the back, spine, and shoulder blades committed to memory years ago. Years ago they would both be awake, watching *Attack of the Giant Leeches* or *Atom Age Vampire* or Cedar's favourite, *The Reptile*. The cold-blooded curse of the girl in the film, a village maid, a doctor's daughter. At dusk, she'd shed her dress and skin for scales. Cedar hasn't really thought about that story in a long time. Now she wants to be her, shifting from girl to monster, sliding in and out of her corset, ever unsuspected. Sinking teeth deep into throats.

Cedar stands by the windows overlooking Riverside Drive, the reflection of Detroit's luminous Art Deco skyline — Cadillac Tower, the Fisher Building, One Woodward Avenue — shining in the river. She looks east, to see if she can glimpse Franco's restaurant, Arrivederci. Though it would be closed now, anyway, she sees nothing but the shingle collage of rooftops, dark blotches of trees. The sky in the east notched with a strange, searing light.

Before the fire ever starts, there is Jules.

Franco would never have hired Jules, but Angela, his best waitress, said *Please*, sliding his resume over the bar. *He's my cousin.* So Franco gave him a chance.

Jules turned out all right. Punctual, energetic, a good waiter. Customers loved him. There is no accounting for taste, Franco sadly knows. People love canned noodles, too, and that was basically Jules: the human equivalent of Zoodles.

Jules is Jäger Bombs and diamond earrings. Jules is putting flame decals on a good car. Jules is Taco Bell for breakfast. Jules, who loves hot reptiles and has theories on Bigfoot, drinking cough syrup and failing chemistry while Franco was star of the school's hockey team, scoring hat tricks and scholarships, studying business and the culinary arts.

Jules is lucky.

These are all the things Franco believes of Jules, and some of them are true, or all of them are true. Now Jules is also an arsonist. Franco knows this too.

When he calls the police, Franco won't press charges for the stolen ring.

When you start letting the smeared mascara stay under your eyes after you cry, that's when you know it's a problem. Cedar knows this, but she doesn't clean her face. She stays like that, looking like 1970s Ozzy Osbourne singing 'Paranoid', lashes gummed together, batwing thick.

Cedar goes to family dinners with Franco. Everyone talks about keeping their weight down and their bank account up. His parents' house on Lake St Clair with its water views, boat dock, the mahogany hardwood and sculptured glass fixtures. His mother, Claire, owns a yoga studio and posts about #fitnessgoals. She still fits into her wedding dress from 1979, snow-white organza. She likes to bring it up over dinner, and also how Cedar doesn't fit into her own wedding dress anymore, A-line beaded ivory.

Cedar says, *If I had got the corset option it would*. But she had gone instead for the row of little white buttons up the back like a beaded spine, and Claire says, *That isn't the point. The point is that you should take care of yourself.* Then she says *Franco, this dinner*, which is cold-water lobster tail and drawn butter, wilted arugula, blistered tomatoes. Franco clarifies his own butter. *Every time, you outdo yourself*, Claire says, laying her knife down on the linen napkin, stainless-steel flatware in matte gold. Cedar thinks of *The Great Gatsby*, how this is what would have happened if Tom had married Myrtle. Not a romance or a tragedy, just long, slow disquiet, and Myrtle forever mixing up the salad fork with the fish fork. Or maybe she would have learned, one day, how to discern the difference.

Cedar and Franco live on the water, too, further west. Neutral monochromatics and ash wood floors. One day, he says, they will have a boat dock and a boat. He already has a name for the boat: *Good Intentions*. Cedar always feels cold on the water.

At least Cedar's the one that got pregnant, Shay says.

Franco doesn't want to go to Cedar's family dinners either. *What does that mean?*

Shay only smiles, picks at her salt-roasted beet salad.

Franco knows what it means. It means Angela. Just because Shay saw them that one time together, at the mall, she thinks she knows, but she doesn't. Like her sister, she eats salad with the wrong fork. The vinaigrette is wildflower honey, but Franco wonders why he bothers. He might as well just bring a bottle of ranch, let them drown it all in soybean oil and sugar.

When Franco thinks about Cedar, he thinks about the good life he's given her, the beautiful house, the sunken living room with the view of the river, the new leather sectional sofa (the grey shade called fin), and it makes him happy. He understands why people start sanctuaries for sick tigers, for greyhounds retired from racing. It's a nice feeling. It's not his fault she never stopped wanting to shotgun a six-pack of Coors, stay up all night watching *Creature From the Black Lagoon*. It's not his fault he did grow up, either. Just like Angela was not his fault, or not entirely. But Franco has ambition; he will keep trying to culture Cedar, gradually, with patience: like an oyster grinding sand into pearls. Making something elegant and pure out of a mess.

A late summer storm snaps the stalks of Cedar's sunflowers. They bend at the waist, faces in the dirt. Taking a roll of duct tape, she goes out with a pair of scissors, tapes their long stems one by one back up against the wall.

Franco's car pulls into the driveway. He gets out, stares at Cedar for a moment, standing there in her pyjama pants, roll of tape round her wrist.

What are you doing?

Fixing the sunflowers.

With duct tape?

It's working.

That's not the point. He never liked sunflowers anyway, lowbrow, flashy flowers. He would like to see something small, neat, disease-resistant—a sleek green boxwood, sharply trimmed.

What is the point?

I wasn't going to say it.

You can say it.

The point is I give you this beautiful home, he says. *And you treat it like trash.*

When Cedar answers the door, she doesn't recognize Jules at first. He is standing there in a yellow hoodie with a snake on the back, hands in his pockets, waiting. When she's seen him before he's in his button-up shirt, white, looking like it would crack like eggshells if you touched it.

Is Franco home?

No.

I'm supposed to pick up his extra keys.

He left them on the table. The sleeves of his hoodie are rolled back to his elbows. Cedar can see the tattoos he covers for work—roses, black stars, the start of angel wings. She can just see the first few feathers. All morning she has been crying, on and off. *Hormones,* Franco says. When she was still working, at an office, there was a workshop about interpersonal relationships, problem solving. The only thing she remembers is the speaker saying you could stop yourself from crying if you kept your butt clenched. Cedar experimented, and it worked, sort of. But the problem is you can't go around clenched up all day. Cedar knows this. She's tried.

Jules can see the dry tracks of tears on her face, like the rivulets rain leaves on dusty glass. *I like your sunflowers.*

Thank you. She pulls her sweater over the second-trimester slope of her stomach, smudges with knuckles at the mascara damp under her eyes. The television is on, *The Reptile. Did you want to come in?*

Alright, he says. *I don't work for an hour.*

Jules walks inside. Cedar shuts the door. *Can I see your wings,* she asks.

Jules is showing up late to work, calling in sick, things he has never done. Franco pulls him aside before his shift starts. *What's going on?*

Jules thinks Franco is emotionally scarred, or maybe he means emotionally stunted. Either way. He is handsome in a sociopathic way, with a cool blankness to him, like the smooth numberless face of his gold watch.

I know, I'm sorry, I've been losing track of time. I've been seeing this girl—

Franco laughs. *You're a hopeless romantic.*

Hopeful romantic.

That isn't the saying.

It's my saying, Jules says. *I'm rewriting the language.* His white dress shirt is unbuttoned and Franco can see his Ed Hardy shirt underneath, a green snake twisting around roses. Shirts like that were a joke ten years ago, and now they're just tragic. Like Jules, a tragic sort of joke. He says, *But she's with someone else.*

Franco says, *Look, Jules, some people are like chicken pox—it's best to have them once and get over it.*

But chicken pox stays in your body forever, Jules says. *It remains in your nerve cells.*

I don't think that's true.

It comes back as shingles, Jules says. *It's painful.*

Alright, Franco says. *My point is, you need to inoculate yourself against some people. Expose yourself in small doses. Like a vaccination for measles. Once or twice, three times maximum. Then you're immune.* The trick is not to overdo it. Franco knows it is solid advice that he's giving;

it's how he got over Angela. His body is now as resistant to her as it is to tetanus.

I don't think you're supposed to talk about people that way.

What way?

Like a virus, Jules says. *Like diseases.*

Franco shrugs. *Look, Jules*, he says. *I just need you to show up for work on time.*

In September, Franco sits with Angela in his car.

Thanks for hiring Jules, she says. *This job has helped him so much. He's so happy. And he's seeing someone now, too.*

There's someone for everyone, I guess.

I want to meet her, but he won't let me. He keeps saying not yet. It's complicated. She's pregnant —

Jules is somebody's father?

Angela says, *It's someone else's.* Her muted-grey, new-manicured nails. The two tiny gold bars of her earrings, slim as pins. She is dressed for work still, the knee-length black pencil skirt, the white blouse cuffed tidily at her elbows. The thin line of gold over her collarbone where her necklace from him catches the light.

That would be so like Jules, Franco thinks. Jules is so messy, like the trashy daytime talk shows on every afternoon in the nineties. Franco can imagine the kind of girl who would end up with Jules but doesn't want to say it. It's a nice night, why ruin it. Maybe Cedar is right, anyway, and sometimes he is too negative. Angela lays her head down on his shoulder, flicks a finger at the radio. Earlier they worked on a new recipe, tagliatelle in a brown butter sauce with parsnips and fried sage; Angela chopped the herbs and now she smells like sage, his favourite.

He says one of these days, though, he wants me to meet her. That we can get together and watch her favourite movie. Something called The Lizard?

The Lizard?

Oh, no, I mean The Reptile.

Franco tells himself he should not be surprised. Cedar is a scavenger, and they take what they can get. Vultures picking at the bone, shiny beetles in dead leaves, foxes by the roadside, licking blood from their fur.

Cedar isn't the only one who wants to cry all day, but the difference between them is that he doesn't. There are other differences, too, but Franco considers this the most crucial one. Maybe this isn't the life he wanted, either, but you make the most of it. Maybe he didn't want to take on the restaurant, his father's business, work seven days a week. Maybe he wanted to be a lawyer or a pastry chef or just a lazy deadbeat like Jules, blowing his pay cheques on tattoos and Red Bull. Or maybe this is what he would have chosen anyway, in the end, but it's the choice itself he wanted, and what he never got.

Now he's sitting in his office just behind the bar, waiting for Jules. He already has the fuel, and has been saving newspapers for a week. Ducking into the library on his lunch break to do a little discreet research. He knows better than to Google the bad things you're about to do, learned as much from his old *Law & Order* marathons with Cedar.

When Jules shows up, he looks nervous, but Franco smiles, offers him a glass of rye, gestures to a chair.

You wanted to talk to me?

I want us to make a trade, Franco says. *I already know what you want. Now I just have to tell you what it is I need.* Twists the wedding ring off his finger, fourteen-carat gold, offers it. A certain percentage of the insurance money too, of course, when all that is sorted out.

Jules doesn't sit, but he listens. When he turns to leave, he shakes Franco's hand, takes the duffel bag Franco has prepared.

Franco walks Jules to the door. *Jules, wait.*

Jules turns around.

The key is multiple ignition points, Franco says.

Franco has read the criminal code; he expects Jules will get four years, five years, maybe two years less a day. He feels like a mad scientist or Dracula in one of Cedar's horror movies, regarding his creation with sorrow, and with pride. He has made a monster, but he has also given Jules a kind of purpose. In a way, it's the second time Franco has given Jules a chance. Someone like Jules always had the urges towards criminality and self-destruction. It is only raw talent Franco senses, the potential for vocation. When Jules does get out, he could make a career of this, if he has enough ambition. It's what Franco would do, if he could.

THE ECHO OF LIGHT FOOTSTEPS ON PARCHMENT

Kimberley Aslett

Kimberley Aslett *is a medical librarian from Northern Ontario, mostly. New to writing, she explores small moments and big feelings in her short fiction. In the past few years, she's been able to experience amazing moments dog-sledding on Lake Lebarge, riding a hot-air balloon over Cappadocia, Turkey, and skating over wild ice on Lake Superior. 'The echo of light footsteps on parchment' was an honourable mention for the 2021 Bumblebee Flash Fiction Contest.*

THE ECHO OF LIGHT FOOTSTEPS ON PARCHMENT

A large book with parchment pages is lying on the oak table, and you could reach out and touch it with a light finger if you wished. On it is a list of deaths in the parish, a parish that exists in name only now, on maps. The lettering is curled like tendrils of plant material, dried and falling to dust. The deaths are from fever, falls, apoplexy, trampling. Cholera. The deceased are young, mostly. Around the letters and numbers that mark the lives, there are marks on the edges of the page, like a tiny furry creature has made its way around the stories of the deaths, walking through the ink of the lives before it dried.

It might be hard for you to imagine the time when the parchment was half-blank, the year of mud roads and coaches and precarious life. In that year, a barefoot child followed a man on his journeys to the various barbers' and doctors' and parish churches where the bodies were taken. The child could follow the flowing black cloak easily, as it was brushed clean and made of a tightly woven wool, and a much better quality than the occupants of most streets would be likely to wear. If you dreamed this man, you would see his home as a place of stone and wood and tapestry and books, of food prepared by a cook and fires lit by a thin girl who would later eat from a wooden bowl in the kitchen.

The man with the dark cloak was one who carried the ink and blotting cloth and the book of parchment, carried the authority of money and status and education. In a sad moment only months before, he had witnessed the name of his wife being written by the priest, who blessed her and the still mound of her belly in her shroud. Her name was with those first few who died of this cholera outbreak.

The child who followed past the market and the animals had received no education but shared hot, simple meals in his dwelling until the parents had died, the father of a fall years before and the mother of the recent disease. The child was often cared for by neighbours and slept inside most nights. In the daylight hours, the child would wander the streets looking for small treasures, like coal that could be burned or a stick in the shape of a person. The clothes on the child looked too short but not too tight.

The man who was inscribing the names of the deceased to keep the records had not written the name of the child's mother, but he might have if she had died only weeks later.

When the man in the cloak finally noticed the child, he remarked on the large eyes, the sombre face, but he was solitary and had no friend to share this with. Instead, he marked the place where the child stopped to watch and left a bun there, like he was feeding a larger bird. He ran his fingers down the list of names, noting the names of women who might have held this child whilst the child was being christened. If you can imagine that he thought of the mound of belly when he saw the child alone, you are helping to weave a story that could have bound them together.

As you scan the list of names, you see the cholera will disappear for a while, and then it will reappear later.

The hand that wrote the names changes over time too. In the spring of the cholera, the man writes nearly all the names. Then in the summer, you will see that there is a change in the hand for weeks at a time. Where has the man gone? Has he left the city? Has he gone alone, or did he decide to bring along a child who might benefit from the sea air? You could touch the script and think of the stones of a shore where a child can watch the birds screech and the waves toss foam like joy. You can imagine the past and the future and the constant of waves and wind and loss and names unremembered and hands that reach across the distances of their world and write nothing but touch each other with comfort.

THE SWITCH FAIRY

Monica Wang

Monica Wang has fiction in Southword and other publications. In 2021 she received scholarship offers for an MA in Creative Writing from the University of Kent and the University of Exeter. Born in Taichung, Taiwan, she grew up in Taipei and Vancouver, Canada, and has spent the past four years in Germany and the Netherlands.

The Switch Fairy

"Please stop pulling on that," the small voice whined. "My leg."

I stopped knitting. I lived alone — someone must've hidden their phone, or themselves, in my apartment. Readjusting my grip on my needles so they could pierce intruder eyes, I checked the sofa. Under the sofa. Around the coffee table. The bare floor? Nothing. I did not own much furniture.

The voice grew louder. "Ow. Ow, you're still pulling. You're giving me rope burn!"

Rope? I kicked over the bag of yarn I'd just brought home and crushed the nearest ball in one fist. Nothing. The next ball. Nothing. The next. Noth — Something crisper than discount yarn poked through the strands and between my fingers: long, thin insect wings. Ew. I tried to hurl the yarn across the room. It flopped a metre away, weightlessly.

From beneath the yarn, a tiny, muffled screech.

"My leg! Had you freed me properly, I would have made today a most glorious, luck-filled day for you. But now!" A daddy long legs, a humanoid daddy long legs, crawled out of the yarn.

"What are you? What is this? Are you a — " I squinted. Perhaps the bug comparison would offend. " A yarn fairy?"

Even at this distance, the disdain was obvious in their face. "You think I came from filthy polly-ester?"

"Hey, no need to be a snob. I just meant I don't exactly have a garden in here. Why are you in my apartment?"

Having pushed the tangled section of yarn down to their ankles, the fairy stretched. The ligaments in their wings collapsed inward, stretched outward. They looked into my eyes. I didn't expect to be so intimidated by something I could crush with a clay yarn holder. (Yeah, the lumpy clay yarn holder. I made it myself.)

"You don't have much of *anything* in here. Not even heating."

Without breaking eye contact with the judgey bug, I crab-walked to the window and closed it. So much for fresh air.

"Since you inquired about my origins," said the fairy.

"I don't think I in —"

"I was born mere hours ago in a smile of pure joy. Before my wings could fully unfurl, you bumbled by with your cheap yarn and caught me by the leg."

"Me? Walked by? Was this at the department store?"

"When a child gazes upon the object of their fervent desire, when a smile blooms across their face …"

I thought of the other shoppers. Their blank or annoyed or somehow both blank and annoyed faces.

" — burst into existence like a brilliant star! I, a delicate" — the fairy clawed at the tangles — "dewdropped" — spit flew from their lips — "rose!"

"So you're a gaming console fairy?"

"A what-sole?"

"Guy in the computer section yelling about missing pre-orders? *His* smile?"

"His smile and joy——"

"Guy in his thirties getting a toy from his elderly parent while giving minimum-wage retail workers a hard time?" Was I the judgey bug? No, no, I couldn't possibly be.

Their voice rose to mosquito pitch. "Will you free me or not?"

"I didn't say I wouldn't. Though if that's the way you ask for help, maybe not?" I gave the sewing scissors a twirl before making the first cut.

"Pray don't take it out on me just because you won't finish knitting this for many more winters."

I felt warm at last. "You probably don't know anything because you were born today, but there's a lot going on in the world and in my life, and I don't have time——"

"Gently with the shears!"

I made the last snip. "There. Fly free or whatever."

"Heartfelt thanks," said the fairy, nasally and without thanks. "Would you like me to grant a wish?"

"Sure. How 'bout the next new gaming console?"

"How about a haircut? Your bangs are a nauseating sight!" They shot into my hair, pulling, biting, and apparently—too fast for me to see in real time—tying tiny knots.

"I cut them myself! I'm a self-reliant adult!" My dry, rough hands caught my own hair instead of the pest and tore out strands.

The fairy laughed, their voice like music. Horror movie violin music. "I shall have a wonderful day after all!"

They shimmered across my living room–kitchen and hovered above the stove. "Take this gift as thanks. Stay warm, stay healthy, goodbye!" Long wings vanished up the ventilator.

"A gift?"

My knitting, my stiff trapezoid of admittedly cheap yarn, with holes marking each time I'd set it down and resumed in the wrong direction, lay complete: a long, slender scarf with dainty bobbles trembling at each end. They reminded me of woodlice.

"It was supposed to be a toque," I whispered.

Silently I wished the fairy a happy life, wherever the kitchen fan led — a dead end in the ceiling, I was told, but the landlord might have been wrong. Then I turned off the lights so they wouldn't be drawn, moth-like, back into my home.

FATE OF CHICKENS

Krista Jane May

Manitoba born and raised, Krista Jane May currently splits her time between Eastend, Saskatchewan, and Vancouver Island following several years on the East Coast. Her work appears in The Antigonish Review, having placed second in the 2018 Sheldon Currie Fiction Prize competition, and in CommuterLit. She was awarded second place in the 2019 Lorian Hemingway Short Story Competition, and was shortlisted for the Pulp Literature's 2020 Raven Short Story Contest and The Fiddlehead's 2020 Fiction Contest. Most recently, her story 'Tiny Sores' was longlisted for the 2021 CBC Short Story Prize.

*F*ate of Chickens

"Plucked chicken," she told William as he headed up the stairs to bed. Not loud enough for him to hear, of course. He'd only accuse her of being drunk, which she likely was. He was probably already disgusted, but it didn't take much these days; or perhaps—and perhaps this was worse—he wasn't thinking about her at all.

"Plucked chicken," she whispered to the empty street from her perch just inside the enclosed front porch, the door cracked open just enough to accommodate the slender bare legs she extended across the wide top step and her need to inhale the thrill of a near-tropical early autumn rainstorm. *Plucked chicken.* Where had that come from, after all these years? It could only have been the sight of those two women strolling down the otherwise deserted 11 p.m. pavement, rainwater rushing stream-like on either side of the slightly raised debris-built-up centre where they'd walked in a cursory attempt to stay dry, avoiding—of course—the elevated and therefore relatively puddle-less sidewalk that flanked only *her* side of the street. Distorted by the filter of the squalling rain-mist beneath the spotlight of the lone overhanging streetlight, their image briefly conjured a moving Renoiresque painting; this vision-like emergence of the two animated figures—as though entering a stage — had submerged Lorena into a painful longing that threatened to simmer on ache. Yet the well-past-middle-aged pair — one scrawny in a jaunty massive-flower-embellished flapper cap, the other portly with long white hair lifting in the gusts that rendered futile the umbrellas they were fighting to control — couldn't be more incongruous to the two young women who insisted on intervening, their superimposed image crowding Lorena's agitated state of consciousness. *Where are you now, Muriel?*

"Plucked chicken?" It was so real, the warmth of her gentle voice, the concern in Muriel's intense black-rimmed Viking eyes. Lorena picked up her wineglass from the veranda floor and took a sip, savouring the images that had arrived as though loosened and torn by the swirling wind from a page of time's scrapbook to settle, then lift again as she tried to gather them all at once and hold them to her breast in her sudden need. Muriel: tall and slender, a river of long dark-blonde hair (so refreshingly unadulterated in those big-hair-crazed times) spilling in tributaries over that well-worn studded black leather jacket that was as natural a part of her as her permanently wind-burned cheeks.

Lorena nodded, agreeing with her perceptive friend as if it made perfect sense to be having this conversation that transcended both time and place, as if they'd both just returned after an extra-long weekend spent home with their families — in Muriel's case a working farm in the province's Interlake district — and were catching up on a Tuesday morning before classes.

"Plucked chicken ... Oh, yes."

It was a mere whisper, yet Lorena aimed her voice in the general direction the women — chattering, absorbed, oblivious — had headed before moving beyond the range of the streetlight's beams, disappearing shadow-like around the next corner. The two hadn't even looked at her house, with its bold-red-lettered "sold" sign flapping in the wind on the tiny front lawn like an unacknowledged fan applauding their grand performance from an inferior theatre seat. Come to think of it, she suspected the women *had* been coming home from a local stage production. In fact—based on what she knew of them—they probably had starring roles in the performance that was currently playing at the Edwardian-era theatre two blocks over on the tiny town's main street. Cloaked in what she had come to think of as carefully applied layers of whimsy—all fluttery gold-embossed skirts and airy sequined scarves—they'd been buoyant as they'd splashed along, no doubt fuelled by a raucous curtain call from their loyal small-town admirers and an internal sense of righteousness. Oh, it was nothing personal, they'd allow themselves, if they gave Lorena and William any thought at all. Devastating a stranger's life never is *personal.*

"Plucked chicken," she reiterated, nodding slowly—thoughtfully—at the empty street, as if it, too, had asked her how she was feeling. As if it were concerned about any reaction she might have to the blatant indifference, the exclusive camaraderie the women flaunted as they carelessly stretched the boundaries of even *their* uncontested domain, no matter if their apparent unabashed joy was magnified in Lorena's mind by the wine. It was the sheer audacity of it; Lorena knew those women just well enough to hope they hadn't spotted her in this pathetic state, furtively eyeing them from her unlit porch. And yet, why should that be? It was they who should be ashamed.

The night was so inviting in its warm, wet hostility; Lorena felt a sudden and overwhelming urge to dance herself, right out there in the island the rushing water had created in the middle of the narrow, wind-crazed street. But even now—even in this dreamlike, inebriated state, with the street so empty now—she was conscious of the possibility of being disastrously observed should she succumb to such an impulse. There were, after all, people on the other side of those neighbouring windows, curtained though they were against the night: people who would—some even could—claim innocence in the ordeal but could not be expected to suppress the natural human urge to add such fresh, juicy fodder to the composting heap of adulterated truths that had once been pure and earmarked for dreams. Even worse—however unlikely—would be the unsavoury consequences she'd face should William take the notion to peek through a slat in the blinds of the upstairs bedroom window. Any dance—any indication of public drunkenness—would disturb William, but the dance beat that had begun to throb within her was like a call to action, a dance of battle, though she was well aware she'd long since yielded to defeat.

"I feel dangerous." Muriel, back then, could utter just those three words, and the excitement that ignited amongst the rest of them would be palpable; beer might be involved in great quantities, perhaps at some unmentionable dark establishment frequented by irresistible, mysterious characters who may well have evolved from the very myth that had given birth to Muriel. It could just as likely happen, though, right there in the sheltered structures of the campus during a Friday afternoon beer bash in, say, the third floor of the Sciences Department where the wide elevator would deposit them into the noisy throng of a suds-slick dance floor. You just knew, the moment you glanced across the huge darkened room, past hundreds of life-crazed decompress-ing youth to a corner where she'd be dancing trancelike to Billy

Idol as he was dancing with himself, and the poor unsuspecting clod who thought *he* was dancing with her just couldn't have a clue, that anything might happen.

Elbowing the door to allow a wider opening, Lorena stretched her legs further outside, dug her bare heels into a gap between two planks, and, in a toddler-style manoeuvre, drew her knees up and dragged her butt onto the outer landing, exposing her whole body now to the seductive elements that the beams of the street-light opposite magnified like an outdoor public video screen. She shrugged off her faded-rose bathrobe, tossing it back onto the veranda before it could get soaked, reached back inside for her wine glass, and took a defiant swig. She wondered—absurdly—if anyone looking might possibly see her as alluring, her still quite youthful figure draped as it were in a sheer, rapidly drenching, blood-red sleeveless nightgown, her wearing features and fading hair disguised by the diminished illumination of the hour.

"I love your eyes," Muriel had told her one ordinary day as they sat across from one another in a darkened booth of the second-floor university centre bar. It had been just the two of them that late afternoon, cold half-pints on the table in front of them. The beer, Lorena remembered, had relaxed her in a wonderful way. She'd loved this new city life away from the high school pecking order of the small steel-mill town she'd grown up in. Alcohol had still been a fun new acquaintance in those days; she hadn't imagined it would one day transmute into the occasionally welcome but often burdensome long-term houseguest she vowed in stronger moments she'd summon the courage to send packing. But back then, it had allowed her to reciprocate Muriel's startling compliment (confession?) casually and with an air of equality she normally wouldn't have allowed herself.

"And I love *your* eyes. Always have." While Lorena had what others had described as big soft dreamy eyes — the kind that she knew, often betrayed a heartfelt and willing loyalty — Muriel had ice-fire Scandinavian blue eyes, dark sapphires reflecting thrilling adventure and peril. Yet she knew instinctively in that moment that Muriel was sincere. Muriel wouldn't need the alcohol, but she would perceive that Lorena might in order to accept this compliment (admission?) without embarrassment, with a grace Muriel had detected in her long before Lorena had matured enough to recognize and appreciate such qualities in herself. The truth was, she'd been stunned by the suddenness of their mutually acknowledged admiration.

"Even on that first day?"

Muriel had laughed lightly as she'd asked, but penetrating, questioning eyes had betrayed something more serious, and Lorena found herself wondering after all these years if she'd missed something vital. She would never forget the first day she'd been introduced to Muriel in Campo — a food court of sorts in the university centre — by a mutual friend. Muriel — so smooth in that second skin of a bad-girl jacket — had studied Lorena with riveting deep-set eyes that could slay. And they nearly had when, finally, she broke what was becoming an uncomfortable silence.

"That is ... without a doubt ... the most hideous sweater I've ever seen."

It's hard, at eighteen — after a less than stellar high school experience one is eager to leave behind for a new life with a reinvented (or perhaps just comfortably revealed) personality — to be so brutally singled out and criticized, especially in a group, some of whom had known her in that ostensibly discarded previous world. Yet in that brief moment, before not-yet-formed tears needed stifling and before there was time to wonder if the misery that was her life would never end, Muriel spoke again, upending any threatening anguish with three miraculous words.

"I *want* it."

And she had flashed her the most wicked, exclusive grin—more eyes than mouth—that had enveloped Lorena like no mere embrace ever could, thus igniting an intimacy of friendship she would never quite comprehend yet would hold sacred for a lifetime.

"Yes," Lorena now repeated through vaporized decades. "Even that first day." *Oh, Muriel. Why did I keep letting you go?*

Behind her—beyond the enclosed porch—in the parlour room adjacent to the small entry hall that contained the painstakingly refinished maple staircase William had so distastefully ascended, there were moving boxes stacked two deep; more boxes lined the walls of the dining room and kitchen. Evidence of a dream shattered, a wearing down of spirits that had culminated in a decisive, irrevocable action after years of torment but ultimately executed before the losses they'd suffered could become so much more than financial. That the women—one of whom would soon *own* this house—hadn't so much as glanced in its general direction as they'd walked by was astonishing—an insult, really. But then, she supposed, why would they? Lorena and William's lovingly restored old home was nothing but an investment for Avril, the larger and evident leader of the two.

"Put a knife in and twist it," she could hear Muriel say, matter-of-fact but presented with a look of fierce solidarity. It was an expression Muriel would often use when one of their group was agonizing over an issue, and not once had it been necessary to begin with "they might as well just ..." Muriel's compact way of affirming that she was on your side—that whatever injustice had been done to you was the worst that could happen—was always more comforting than lengthy, rehashed "poor you" discussions in which the rest of their tittering group indulged. Yet Muriel—a little older than most of them in years and much older in so many other ways—had rarely been forthcoming with her own personal troubles. Lorena suspected there had been problems she herself hadn't been mature enough to perceive, wrapped up as she'd been with her own making-up-for-high-school woes. There'd of course been hints, but hadn't Muriel seemed content to leave it that way? Or had Lorena—ill-equipped in her naivety—been too afraid to delve deeper, thus avoiding her own risk of exposure?

She picked up her wine glass, set it back down, wondered if it was worth risking the alert of the squeaky floorboards to go to the kitchen for a refill. They'd taken a hard loss on the house in the end, finally handing it over to a real estate agent with a rock-bottom, non-negotiable price attached that was sure to see quick results after years of yo-yoing strategies colliding with seesawing emotions. Lorena loved their quaint seacoast-town abode in spite of the toxic atmosphere they'd found themselves living in, and she'd clung to a hope that either the situation would resolve or—at the very least—they'd find a buyer who would appreciate the love and care that had gone into the restoration of the beautiful character home. That the local, flippant new owner had put in her offer the minute the *For Sale by Owner* sign had been switched to the real estate company's branding had been the final twist of that knife; Lorena wondered if she'd bleed internally forever, while William was just glad it was finally over.

An early image of Muriel materialized, so vivid the fresh wind brought an incongruous whiff of a long-extinguished *Player's*

Extra Light: Muriel arriving at Campo one morning, a look of sheer disgust on her face as she picked at her jacket and jeans with her slender long fingers. Lorena had raised her eyebrows in question, and Muriel had revealed something of a chore-filled weekend spent home at the farm; apparently there hadn't been time to change after a load of freshly slaughtered chickens had been delivered from the back seat of the station wagon she'd shared on the ride back to the city with the brothers who were delivering the chickens somewhere along the way. It had been an exaggeration, of course — there hadn't really been any feathers stuck to her — but the gesture of plucking at her jacket had struck Lorena as particularly expressive. A few mornings later, following an exam she'd been ill-prepared for, Lorena had met Muriel for coffee and, in answer to her "How did it go?" had mimicked the manoeuvre, plucking here and there at her now-prized hideous wool sweater. Muriel had smiled and squeezed her hand in understanding. After that, in certain overwhelming personal circumstances where talk proved difficult, "plucked chicken" became the only phrase required.

Lorena considered again the empty street; the storm still raged, and she longed to toss back another glass of wine, dance with abandon with Muriel beneath the streetlight. She pictured the two of them out there, the raindrops ricocheting off Muriel's leather armour but soaking into her own inadequate cover of a double-breasted navy wool sweater with a wide collar and two rows of coin-like buttons. A long-ago midweek evening when Muriel had invited her to an underground punk bar in a seedy section of Winnipeg, it had just been the two of them. Prior to entering the dimly lit premises that pulsed a thrilling underworld aura even up on the street, Muriel had asked Lorena if she'd mind switching her sweater for Muriel's jacket. Lorena remembered being a combination of bewildered, exhilarated, and nervous but trying to betray none of these feelings. Lorena remembered watching Muriel that evening as she danced, the buttons on that ridiculous grade-school-girl sweater flashing seductively under the strobe lights. Had she wanted to feel what it was to be Lorena? Had she wanted Lorena to somehow absorb what it was like to be her? Perhaps it had been her way of trying to say that clothes were nothing more than just that—clothes. Or perhaps it had been simply a whim, meaning nothing at all. She'd never dared ask Muriel, perhaps out of fear of some truth she didn't wish to face yet, but she'd always felt a deep gratitude. The thrill had been real but had dissipated once she'd realized—with surprising relief—that nothing was going to be altered simply by masking herself for those few hours in the very essence of Muriel. It had been a comfort to slip back into her familiar old cardigan.

Rising from her sopping perch, Lorena stood tall, shook the rain from her shoulders, and spread her wings before the luminous vision. And there, within the comforting certainty of the persistent rain, she was hit with a flash of lucidity: the truth was so clear in that stormy atmosphere that she began to laugh without fear.

"Thank you, Muriel," she whispered to the swirling wind, knowing somehow, somewhere, Muriel would think of her and smile.

But nothing changes, not really—especially if you keep going back. Solidarity with William was one thing she still had, and right now, she would do what was required to hang on. She suppressed the primal urge to join Muriel beneath the mist-obscured streetlight and, after watching just a little while longer, Lorena slipped inside and left her dancing there alone.

PALE PONY EXPRESS

Lulu Keating

Lulu Keating has been writing short fiction and screenplays since the early 1980s. Klondike Kalahari won the screenplay competition in the Vancouver International Women in Film Festival, 2021. Two recent stories were shortlisted for the BC Yukon Flash Fiction Contest in 2020. Her writing has been published in Geist, The Globe and Mail, North of Ordinary, and What's Up Yukon. Originally from Antigonish, Nova Scotia, Keating now makes her home in Dawson City, Yukon Territory, where she continues to write short fiction and work on her third novel. 'Pale Pony Express' was an honourable mention in the 2021 Bumblebee Short Story Contest.

$\mathcal{P}$ALE PONY EXPRESS

The little girl asks me for the story. Her blonde ringlets hang to her shoulders. She's old enough to hear the truth. I reel myself back, return to the woman I was before she took root.

It had been twenty days since we'd talked about it. Time was running out.

I suggested, "Let's take a run down to the Pale Pony."

That's what we called Whitehorse.

Rory said, "We only got two days off. You wanna spend six hours each day drivin'?"

"Five," I told him, "if you let me behind the wheel." He won't.

Even when you live offgrid, word gets around. The law of the north is that you can't refuse to help others. They came to us with their lists. Sandy needed a fan for his stove and a hard drive. Rebecca needed pasties for her burlesque. Sarah needed roofing nails. Really, Sarah? Your roof is under three feet of snow.

We were ready to go when Katrina pulled in, blocking us. The bed of her pickup truck had a custom-built dog carrier. Three dogs stuck their heads out of round cubbyholes.

Katrina won't get to it right away. She introduced the dogs.

"Nobody will adopt them until they're fixed."

She'd go herself but she's too busy at the shelter.

"It's all lined up at the vet clinic."

She held out the truck keys.

There was only one cassette in the truck. After one hundred kilometres of Hank Snow, we shut it off. We finally talked about the stillborn (Gertrude). The doctor told us we were unlikely to lose another, but we saw death everywhere. The Klondike Highway was bruised with nightmare landmarks: where I slid off, where Rory crashed. Almost there, we skidded on black ice and bounced off a snow bank. When we finally arrived, we were grim and exhausted. After the errands were done, we agreed we would talk. My pregnancy. We would decide if we'd go through it all again. It was still early enough to make a decision.

The damn vet clinic ordered us back in four hours to pick up the dogs. The pert assistant explained, "This is a freebie for the Dawson shelter. You can't expect us to keep the dogs overnight."

Try sneaking three drugged-up cone-heads into a pet-free motel. I distracted the desk clerk while Rory smuggled. The dogs kept us awake all night with their restless wandering. As soon as we fell into deep sleep, they needed out. That was the start of another nightmare day. The malamute couldn't jump onto the truck bed. Rory lifted him: the dog twisted, nipped Rory, and ripped his stitches. Back to the vet.

By the time we made it home, Rory and I weren't talking. In bed, we chilled each other. In the morning, Rory touched my belly. My hands covered his. Softening, clinging, crying. Tenderness reignited. We melted into each other.

"And that, little girl, is how you came to be."

THE MAGIC SHUFFLING MACHINE

Derek Salinas Lazarski

Derek Salinas Lazarski is a writer and educator in Chicago. His work has been featured in Curbside Splendor, Portage Magazine, Oyster River Pages, *and the* Second Hand Stories *podcast. His writing nosedives into the construction of meaning, the extraordinary in the everyday, and the limits of the heart and the mind. He lives in Chicago with his wife, two children, and two cats. For more of his writing, visit dereksalinaslazarski.com.*

THE MAGIC SHUFFLING MACHINE

I

My sister Kelsey moved in with me the day before the project was assigned. Initially I thought living with her was going to be fun. Pizza and beer and movies every night. Then, a week later, I had no control of the television and the fridge was filled with vegan cheese.

What could I do? Her super-successful pompous cellist husband back in that big philharmonic dumped her second-chair flute for the first-chair clarinet. Couldn't let her move back with Mom and Dad. Mom was still seasoning the cast-iron skillet every day out of calcified routine, and Dad would have her sanding cabinets in the garage. Better she move from the city to a big Midwestern suburb than to a boring rural one.

Also, I had no excuse. For the four or so years before Kelsey moved in, my days had been spent analyzing budgets for Carnetica while at night I was parked at the computer escaping in fantasy RPGs and falling down message board rabbit holes. And, when I could kickstart my motivation, ploughing ahead on the murder mystery library.

That's when Research Project 916-00-3871 landed in my department queue.

All I wanted was a slow Monday. To leave the cube as little as possible.

But, first thing in the morning, there it sat, a new budget line lurking there beneath my other departments like a whitehead pimple: Plastics. Domestics. Auxiliary. And, gods be damned, Research Project 916-00-3871.

Clicking it didn't expand into any detail. The Explanation field held only two words. That's it. No lengthy abstract full of molecules and polymers. No citation list. No inscrutable description.

The two words in the explanation field were this: Occurriential Interdeterminism.

A Google search yielded nothing.

I swivelled to the other cubicle and tapped Bennie on the shoulder. He's the other budget analyst here. Failed out of seminary. Smoked too much weed.

He leaned over and squinted. "Could be anything. A slush fund. Pet project. They throw stuff like that on me all the time."

They did. Most new budgets went to Bennie, who, despite being ten years older than me, was less trustworthy because, I guessed, he had a big bushy ponytail. He managed budgets for the long list of research projects at Carnetica while I watched the budgets of the three major aforementioned departments of Plastics, Domestics, and Auxiliary. Plastics makes parts you don't know exist for your dishwasher and car. Domestics makes department store chaff like candles, pillows, and avocado peelers. Auxiliary has a few special projects embedded in it, like the off-track betting machines we make the shells for, but otherwise comprises some other random stuff and all the overhead, like my pedestrian salary.

I showed him the Explanation field. Occurriential Interdeterminism. Whatever that was.

He shrugged with great difficulty. Then his interest drifted back to the SETI scanner on his right monitor. The scanner was more than a hobby. He told me he went to bed every night sending thoughts to the aliens because he was fairly certain they were listening in on him and coming soon.

"But what about the number?" I asked. "The number of the project?" But when he said what, I said never mind.

My eyes were fixed on it. 916-00-3871. It was my social security number.

Mercer answered immediately. "This can't be happening. My best budget analyst calling *me*? Is there a total eclipse or something?" Then my boss's cheery voice got serious. "There's not a bomb threat, is there? A gunman? Don't tell me you're quitting."

Mercer was two years older than me, ten times more polished, twenty times as perky. "Social security number? Elliot, my man, you know those research project numbers are random generations." He laughed like it was an inside joke. "Security purposes. Why do you ask?"

"What's up with the explanation?" I asked. He waited. "It's word vomit."

"Isn't it all?" His smile oozed through the phone's black plastic. "Listen, do you need anything from me to track expenses? No? You're doing a great job? Then I'm doing a great job, Elliot. Beers on Friday if you and Benzo are in."

Kelsey's stuff was draped all over the futon, the coffee table, the stools at the counter. Sure, it was still all my old college furniture, but now it was covered with clothes, yoga mats, boxes of candles and crystals and miscellaneous bathroom appliances. *Golden Girls* on the TV. Kelsey glued to it, oversized mug of green tea in her hands, oversized college sweatshirt, her flute lying across her lap like a dead pet. She hadn't played since the divorce. Now it was as limp as the rest of her junk filling my apartment. So much for a roommate being fun.

Still, Research Project 916-00-3871 perplexed me so much that I was waving my beer around, happy to have someone to rant to. "Here's something else weird," I droned on to myself, my button-down untucked and halfway unbuttoned. "There are eight budget lines for every department: salaries, benefits, supplies, equipment, et cetera, and the dollar amounts are all different because, duh, these things cost different things."

Her eyes stayed glued to the screen as she said, "This is the most I've ever seen you worked up about anything."

I wanted to yell that despite my perpetual disenchantment, the numbers actually matter, the way the numbers get to be the numbers matters, the reasons these numbers are not other numbers matter. But I ignored her.

"The amounts for this stupid research project? Two hundred and fifty K in every line. Like, what?" Some beer flew out of the bottle. Unnecessary waste. "Carnetica's earmarking two mil for this thing. But the budget lines are irrelevant??"

"Yeah that doesn't make a lot of sense." A laugh track from the television. She turned to me and cocked her head thoughtfully. "Do you have any other work clothes? You wear the same light-grey button-down and dark-grey khakis every day."

"What?"

"I'm just wondering if I'm seeing things or if your closet is just multiple copies of the same outfit. Wait, are you a cartoon character?"

Another snarky comment I chalked up to the divorce. "Who cares? They're just work clothes. I'm content with blending into the walls of the office."

Mercer didn't have any other answers. RP 916-00-3871 must have come from high up, board of directors maybe. You know how these things go.

Then the spending started.

First came the salaries and benefits. The project director moved quick. Had an army of twelve or so scientists working for her already, and once Rhonda in HR hooked me up with their specs, I figured they'd blow through their nonsense budget in a few months. So I emailed Mercer. *Just monitor it* was all he wrote back.

Then there were the purchases. Who knows what the science equipment was? A spiro-this, a chrono-that, a something-graph, a whatever-probe. As a budget analyst, I double-check all the purchasing. That's basically it. Normally we just approve this stuff and then go back to the scientists if we get audited, but the costs were $14K, $27K, $35K. *Anything over $10k needs three competitive quotes*, I wrote to Mercer. *Scientists know math, right?*

Mercer sent a laughing emoji before telling me to *Call the RP director* and throwing in *Does sarcasm belong in a professional email?* which left me wondering if he was being sarcastic or not. But instead of emailing the RP director, I examined the purchases more closely and found them to be different kinds of kits. I was able to avoid getting quotes by breaking them each down into multiple purchases and buying the nonsense parts separately.

Then $75K in other requests machine-gunned into my queue even faster than the reqs from Plastics usually did. Computers, circuit boards, wiring, copper tubing, aluminum sheeting, all of it just ripping through their supply budget. Maybe they were just getting started, but on a hunch I emailed Benediccio, the head of Domestics. She had extra inventory she could lend, mainly the circuit boards and aluminum, allowing us to circumvent these purchases. *Happy to do it*, she wrote. Good budget analysting by me. She added, *Let me know when you want to discuss those management videos I sent you, Elliot!!*

Hadn't yet occurred to her that I wasn't management material. I just manage the comings and goings of dollars on a screen. My preferred professional development was slogging through coding tutorials online when my queue was empty and I'd hit a dead end on the murder mystery library.

And that's when things got really messy: the budget transfer rationales.

"It's foreign to me why you would need to write a rationale for a budget transfer anyway," Kelsey said, pinching a checker piece. We were playing our childhood game, Connect Four, in one of those coffee shops where people with serious beards or purple streaks in their hair sat on their laptops all day. No place like this out by Mom and Dad. "They have the money. Who cares what budget line it's in or why you move it over?"

I dropped a piece in, then started diatribing. Along with a budget being a moral document, I explained, there was the FCC, the SEC, board policies, compliance laws, basic fiduciary responsibility. Things that clearly eluded the myopic scientific mind of the director of RP 916-00-3871, whose name, I learned, was Dr Gloriana Jimenez.

Bennie got her name from HR. Said Dr Jimenez must know someone who knows someone on the board to get a project going with us. Scientist politics. That didn't excuse her from not knowing how to write a proper rationale for moving money from one $250K budget line to another, as if anyone would spend exactly $250K on salaries and equipment and supplies in a single goddamn year. She's a scientist, so theoretically she knows math, and Mercer sent her all the job aids on how to manage your departmental money, and yet here we were a week later with equipment and supply purchases of $54K, $72K, and $92K, and Dr Jimenez, two weeks in, trying to spend from budget lines she'd already drained. So she tried transferring funds from Travel and Meeting Expenses and Other with absurd budget transfer rationales like *No conferences on our topic!* and *We have no need to meet!* and *No other money needed!* Rejected. Rejected. Rejected. None of those explanations specifically described why they weren't going to use the budgeted dollars they were trying to transfer.

But the purchases kept coming, one for $200K, and Mercer must've been feeling pressure from up top because then he told me to ask for money from the Domestics department's Supplies line. Benediccio agreed to loan some of it, $75K. *Part of playing the game, Elliot,* she wrote. *Lessons abound!* But the purchases kept coming, the poorly written rationales kept getting rejected, and then Mercer sent me through the roof by telling me to pull from the Plastics department's Travel line.

Plastics is run by Eccleson. Twice my age, comb-over, two daughters in college, a sneery smile. The kind of guy who still wears his high school ring on his hairy hand. When I finally worked up the guts to email him and ask for money, he replied with one line: *Elliot, is this a mistake or a practical joke?* But Upstairs must've talked to him because, hours later, he emailed saying he approved.

Still Dr Jimenez kept trying to transfer money over what she knew she had, and the rationales kept getting rejected by me and then Mercer and then whoever's above Mercer. I even tried to rewrite them as best I could, but to no avail because I had no clue what Occurriential Interdeterminism was. But after all my complaining, Bennie told me to just walk all the way to the R Building and get the answers from her. Mercer called and declared in the most uninterested tone possible, "Elliot, I am ordering you to speak to Dr Jimenez in person."

Kelsey's eyes betrayed her boredom with my story. Apparently her troubles were bigger than mine. "Then put your big-boy pants on and walk over there already." She dropped a piece into the Connect Four board. Four in a row. "What I wouldn't give to meet someone new right now." Then she unlatched the bottom of the board. All the pieces fell out.

2

A light rain pinged me in the face as I trekked the Carnetica campus, down the B Building escalators, through the lobby, past the coffee shop where I pick up breakfast every morning, out to our parking lot, through the courtyard where the scientists eat lunch on sunny days, past the behemoth buildings for Plastics Moulding and Domestics Assembly, past multiple other Cold War buildings of windowless concrete, past the water tower and Maintenance and the police office, past the new glass lab building, through another parking lot, until, finally, I was at the R Building, my grey khakis damp with drizzle.

At the security desk they directed me down a bunch of long white brick corridors that reminded me of a mental institution. Then I walked through two steel doors into a large new warehouse filled with expensive-looking scientific equipment and tables all around covered with files and notes and doodads. Young scientists in lab coats roamed around. I asked for Dr Jimenez. They directed me to some offices in the corner.

Her small office was jammed with stacks of paper and all manner of little trinkets lining bookcases and shelves: toy cars, dolls, a tiny Statue of Liberty, little ceramic animals, one of those drinking-bird things, a PEZ dispenser, little games, a Superman action figure. Stuff was everywhere.

She came from behind the cluttered desk, about my height, with straight shoulder-length brown hair and tortoiseshell glasses and a little too much lipstick on her pretty smile. A pair of Nikes poked out beneath her lab coat. She was maybe ten years older than me but, despite being exceedingly polite, had the authority of a few more decades.

"Yes, Elliot! Thank you for coming! It seemed like only time before our paths would cross."

Her accent was thick and beautiful, her language elongated, but her enthusiasm wasn't my thing. I got to the point, re-explaining the budget transfer process despite Mercer having done it twice already. I showed her examples of rationales that I'd also email. Then I talked about the $200K she had requested out of nowhere, how I could get $75K of it from Benediccio, but, honestly, I really shouldn't have to because the money was already there in Dr Jimenez's budget, just waiting to be moved around with a proper rationale.

She listened carefully, her pointer fingers pressed against her lips. Then she spoke as if I hadn't said a word. "Please let me explain to you our work." Ridiculously polite. She came around the desk to lead me out, but one of her many trinkets caught my eye. A miniature Connect Four board. "Huh. My sister and I still play this. Our favourite game when we were kids."

Her face lit up at this, then she smiled and nodded, motioning me out into the warehouse.

She brought me to a table with two metronomes standing a few feet apart. "A demonstration. Scientists, we're so abstract. It's so important for us to make the public *understand* what we do." The word *understand* was emphatic. Then she started one of the metronomes. "Can you make the other match?" I shrugged and gave it a try, but they didn't match exactly. "But at some point, they will strike at the same time." She smiled.

"I'm familiar with wave modulation."

She nodded and motioned me to follow her to a different table. There seemed to be no order to anything in the work area: the equipment, the tables, their contents, the motions of the lab assistants. The only thing that anchored the space was a large object in one corner of the warehouse, a hulking machine of dull grey steel near the size of a train engine and covered in knobs and pipes and gauges and wires. I wondered which purchase, or purchases, had created that behemoth.

Now at a different table, she held up a small device, acting like a TV scientist for kids. "Do you know what this is?"

"An automatic playing card shuffler," I said. "My sister and I had one."

"Very good." Dr Jimenez loaded a deck into the shuffler and shuffled. Then she did it again, and again. "One of my boyfriends in college, he was brilliant. Theoretical physicist. Handsome and arrogant." She swooned, rolling her eyes, a hand on the chest of her lab coat. Despite being totally batty, she had her charm.

"We used to do thought experiments. You know thought experiments? He created one of my favourites. Called it the 'Magic Shuffling Machine.'" She held up the shuffler, then kept shuffling the deck with a whirring riffle. "There are two versions of Magic Shuffling Machine. The first is realistic, less fun. The second is theoretical. Extremely fun.

"The first version of Magic Shuffling Machine goes like this: imagine you had every deck of cards in the entire world. You put them in the Magic Shuffling Machine and you shuffle and you shuffle and you shuffle and — poof! — you have every deck in the entire world perfectly randomized."

"Except perfect randomization is impossible," I said.

She held up a finger in front of her knowing smile. "Very good, Elliot. But now let's say you take the top two cards off the deck. What are the odds you get a perfect match? Two copies of the eight of diamonds? How far down do you have to go before you get a match?"

"It's just probability," I said. "There are equations that can figure that out."

"Yes, but I am not speaking of probability, Elliot." Finally she brought out her condescending scientist tone. "I am speaking of coincidence."

"Then that's not scientific," I laughed.

"We'll get back to that. Next I want you to imagine every playing card is a different molecule in the universe."

"That doesn't work either," I countered. "Some molecules just don't interact with others. Spades might play with clubs but completely ignore hearts."

"Yes, yes. And here we see the limits of realistic Magic Shuffling Machine. Now, Elliot," Dr Jimenez continued, setting her fists on her temples. "Imagine a second version of the Magic Shuffling Machine. A theoretical version. A version that can achieve perfect randomization." And her fists exploded out as her eyes opened wide. "How long would you need to shuffle for the top two cards to match? Or, another approach, how far down would I need to go to find a match to the top card?"

"Unanswerable questions," I said, still thinking. "Every answer is possible. With perfect randomization the second card and the infinitely last card are both possible. The pair could be right there or, really, it could never happen."

She nodded the whole time, her lipsticked smile enjoying my thinking. "The odds are so small," she agreed. "And yet"—she opened her arms wide and looked around the warehouse—"look at all we have. How, in all these decks of cards, does one find its match?"

As she walked me to the door, many possibilities popped into my head. There would be infinite copies of the eight of diamonds. Why even find a pair at all? Or why not get *all* of them together? Seemed like the limitations of the question were artificially creating the answers.

As she left me at the steel doors with the politest handshake ever, a scientist came through them from lunch, sans lab coat, in a light-grey button-down and dark-grey khakis. They looked at each other with a smirk before he pointed at my clothes and said, "Nice style."

Then I was alone, my mind racing with even more questions. And I hadn't even asked about Occurriential Interdeterminism.

"So you like her." That was Kelsey's conclusion from my story. Not that, after going all the way out to the R Building to visit a mad scientist, I still knew nothing about the project. "Just make up the budget rationales. No one's going to read them." Her tone of voice suggested she was so over my drama. My sister, who was on the couch in her pyjamas, watching some trashy matchmaking reality show.

I was ranting, waving around a *Murder, She Wrote* DVD case that had a *Columbo* DVD inside. How was I so good at accounting while so many of my cases had the wrong discs in them? Happens so often when you buy them in bulk off the internet.

"Kelsey, every dollar spent is tied to a rationale, which is tied to a strategic plan, and all the spending marches in lockstep to that plan. I know the costs of plastic dials that go on coffee makers. Reservoirs for automobile radiators and the moulds and machinery used to make them. Costs per yard for rolls of plastic sheeting. But I know nothing about this whole project. Clicking that approval button in ignorance means I'm permitting the Wild West. If I allow one random gigantic purchase just because no one is going to know, then how doesn't that invalidate everything I've ever done there?"

"Oh, goddammit, Elliot," she erupted. "I played in front of hundreds of people and made their hearts burst. Burst! Your main form of entertainment is murder! I'm bringing forth life, you're wallowing in literal death." Then she slapped the remote into my hand and grabbed her yoga mat from the corner. "No wonder you're worried about things no one will read!" Then she stormed off to the apartment building hallway, the only place she could get away from me, to downward dog out there.

I pointed *Columbo* at the TV and mumbled, "Maybe you shouldn't subject yourself to this crap, Kelsey." But she was right. I hated her sulkiness but couldn't blame her. She showed no interest in going back to see Mom and Dad on the weekends. She hadn't even told them she was in town.

So fine. If Kelsey wanted to self-isolate, I still had plenty of murder mystery DVDs to rip to my hard drive. And to watch too, I guess.

The next week Dr Jimenez ramped things up quick. Industrial-size generators, solar panels, $25K in helium. A few budget transfer rationales I approved, others I rejected. Mercer again asked me to ask Eccleson for money but backed off when I admitted I was scared of the guy.

I showed Benny. "Helium? She must be throwing a giant birthday party down there," he said, lacking interest. "Or filling a dozen parade floats."

"It's not funny," I said. "There's a helium shortage."

He just shrugged and turned to the Bigfoot documentary he had pulled up on YouTube. One of the many things Bennie has told me was that he literally wanted to find Bigfoot, make a fire with him, just be his friend.

Soon after, Mercer sent me a meeting invite to come see him in his office in C Building. So passive aggressive. When I got there, he was doing yoga on a mat in his office, his tie tucked into his button-down. "Elliot, my man." He looked up, straining. "We've been directed by Upstairs to push this one through."

I went into my spiel about being the budget gatekeeper, all the money marching in lockstep, blah blah. He wasn't hearing it. "Upstairs is behind Jimenez. I'm supposed to green-light everything. Get it from Benediccio or Eccleson, like before."

I pleaded. He should go down to R, learn the project, rein her in. But he cut me off. "Just do it, Elliot. Like Nike." He balanced in crane pose, his hands praying. "Just do it like Nike."

I walked out, my throat in a knot. I called Benediccio first, started politely, then explained about the helium. Told her about all the knickknacks, the disarray. She didn't reciprocate my laughter.

"It's not about the money," was her reply, her tone conciliatory, coaching, wise with age. "This is about knowledge, discovery. Is that a lens you employ, Elliot? My parents didn't. They were working class, raising kids, building cabinets. This paradigm is a luxury we're afforded, the paradigm of pure human knowledge acquisition, and for those of us in research, that drive, that purity, it exists outside — nay, on a higher plane, even — than petty concerns like budgets, politics, even friendship. Do you grok that, Elliot? Do you? The places we uncover in our work are new corners of the cave that the human torch has not yet reached. And, once illuminated, they are accessible to us for now and all time. So, no, this is not about the money. I should hope, in the same way, you're progressing with those coding workshops. You're doing good things, Elliot. Unlocking doors in your mind that will be forever open to you."

I scoffed and said I didn't think the coding would turn into anything and I'd probably be looking at budgets my whole career.

But thanks. And if it wasn't about the money, could I take a hundred grand from her budget?

No. She needed it. But she could give me thirty-five. Then she politely ended the conversation.

I waited all afternoon before calling Eccleson. From the moment he picked up and barked, "Budget boy," I held the receiver three inches from my ear. Benny was busting up.

"Sixty grand?" I could nearly smell his breath through the receiver. "Budget boy wants sixty grand from me to give to some firecracking broad in a lab coat with enough party balloons to fly a tank to the moon? What a joke. What. A. Joke. *Ha.* Tell me, Elliot, do you eat food?"

"Food, sir?"

"Do I have an accent? Yes. Food."

"Ummm." Benny was laughing so hard in the other cubicle his big brown hands covered his face.

"You know who else eats food, Elliot? The hundred and forty-six staff on my payroll. I swear to God, Elliot, I had less than three seconds to waste today and it sure as hell wasn't going to be on you. All I want from you is yeses. Yes yes yes. Otherwise I'll happily talk to Upstairs and get you replaced, Bachelor's Degree. Have you tagging boxes in the warehouse or, better yet, begging for change on the sidewalk. And, no, Mercer can't help you. I've known Upstairs for decades, and they know Mercer is just some young handsome punk with great forearms who is only doing this until he thinks his Bitcoin is worth enough for him to quit. So that's it, Elliot. You're my yes man. All yeses."

I took a deep breath. Then I asked him, if I found the $60K from all his vacant positions and reworked his budget for him, I could give it to Jimenez. He grunted and hung up.

I emailed Dr Jimenez and told her the good news. But when it came time to write out the rationale for the budget transfer, I just stared at the screen.

Kelsey had pulled away. More TV, fewer meals together, fewer coffee shops and Connect Four. Most of my time at home was again spent at the computer, surrounded by stacks of DVDs, though now I felt sequestered.

Another $100K worth of helium sat at the top of my queue. Also a one-line email from Mercer that read, "Take it from Eccleson." My throat knotted itself again, taking the place of the neckties I don't wear. Benny was out because he'd sprained his ankle falling off a ladder getting something for his mom in the kitchen, so I texted him. He told me I should just "Nike it," winky emoji.

I stared at my monitor most of the morning before angrily pulling my jacket on and trudging across campus to Building R. If Mercer wouldn't rein in the project, I figured trying myself would be better than crossing Eccleson again and potentially losing my job, losing my apartment, and sending Kelsey and me both back home to Mom and Dad's, the dreaded purgatory of millennial failure.

The warehouse was buzzing. There were even more tables of random stuff, some scientific and some not, along with more research assistants. The train-engine machine in the corner had been replaced with a massive shining steel ball with long stiff steel prongs projecting in every direction. A stereo blared The Who. 'Pinball Wizard', a song my dad would sing to us before bed.

Winding through the warehouse, I stopped at the sight of a busy scientist wearing a *Terminator 2* T-shirt under his open lab coat. "Awesome." I pointed. "That's my favourite movie." He just pursed his lips, and was nodding knowingly when I felt a touch on my arm.

Dr Jimenez stood there in her lab coat and Nikes and turtle-shell glasses, her hair held up by a pencil.

"Can I take you to lunch, Elliot?" Why not?

She took me to an Italian place downtown called Columbo's. I told her my mom named our dog Columbo after her favourite detective. She said nothing.

After ordering a regular Coke, she asked me to tell her about myself, and I started to wonder if this was a date. With a beautiful eccentric scientist more than a decade my senior. No way. Maybe.

I gave her just surface-level info, but she just kept prying with those polite questions until I found myself reluctantly opening up about my project. "My real hobby ... my project ..." I found myself saying. "I rip DVDs of murder mystery TV shows, crime shows, police procedurals. *Murder, She Wrote, Perry Mason*, Agatha Christies, that kind of thing. We grew up on them in my family, and I just started in high school trying to make a digital library to take to college, and then I guess I just got to trying to push the collection as far as it would go."

"Pirating *Law and Order* and *CSI*?" She smiled conspiratorially, her accent alluring. "Not exactly legal."

"Some pursuits have higher moral standards." Benediccio would be proud. "Problem is I've taken it too far. I'm too completionist. For the last few weeks I've been scouring the internet for a copy of this detective series called *Nero Wolfe*, but it costs a fortune. You know I ordered one and it had a Spice Girls DVD inside? You know how often that happens?"

Both her palms pounded the table. "That would happen all the time in college, when I'd rent them!" I was taken aback by her excitement. "But why murder mysteries, Elliot?"

"I don't know, I guess because the detective always explains everything. All mystery at the beginning, none at the end. They all eventually make sense."

We both ordered Chicken Parmigiana, which I said was the one dish my mom would consistently make at home. When she said, "Me too!" I searched for dishonesty in her voice but couldn't find any.

At this point I was sick of not knowing why I was here. "Tell me about the helium," I said.

"What do you want to know?" Her smile was too genuine to be angry at.

"I need to know about the project. Look, I get that you maybe don't want everyone to know everything, and I don't necessarily need tons of detail in the budget rationales. But the more funding you ask for, the more questions will be asked."

She took a long thoughtful moment before she licked her lips, perhaps wondering how to proceed. I sipped my water.

"Elliot, do you know what the gravity of the sun is?"

I threw my hands up. "I absolutely don't."

"Two hundred seventy-four meters per second. Squared. Twenty-eight times the gravity of the earth."

"So."

"So I am trained as a physicist, but still it astounds me to put a number on this force that binds the solar system together. And not just the solar system, but the Earth! Water, trees, life, school buses and soap operas and Chicken Parmigiana. I was always fascinated by the Triple Alpha Reaction, always in the camp that believed the Hoyle Resonance had more than just a mathematical basis. But how to test it?"

She saw I had no idea what she was talking about.

"So my curiosity pushed me toward the problem from a different angle. You are familiar with Jung's writings on synchronicity? Or Koestler's work? Narrative Vector Dynamics?"

"Occurriential Interdeterminism?"

Her smile relaxed all the muscles in my back. "Exactly. As a scientist, I should be dogmatic about the statistical inevitability of simultaneous occurrences, and yet ..."

"So the Magic Shuffling Machine," I thought out loud, "that big shiny ball in the corner of the warehouse, it's trying to stack the deck? But what does that even mean?"

"We are talking magnetic fields. There's a radius to the emanation ..." Dr Jimenez spread her fingers wide on the table, searching for a coherent explanation. Then she cocked her head and raised her eyebrows, as though deciding something, and when she resettled herself in her chair she seemed the most professorial and authoritative as I had yet seen her. Ironic considering the lack of science in what she was about to say.

"My mother went insane the day my father told her he wanted a divorce." At this I stopped chewing, then forced myself to restart. "Before that, my father and I were close. He hung electrical wires, used to say how clear the stars were from atop a pole. His love of astronomy is why I became a physicist.

"My mother, on the other hand, could not be more different. She was a spiritual-seeker type, did home health visits for elderly, taught yoga on the side. Looking back, I do not know how they wound up together other than my father loved that my mother cooked everything in a cast-iron skillet. I know he always adored her, even at the end. He was just never able to open up in the way she needed.

"One day, she was washing the dishes, incense burning, chanting playing on the stereo. My father walked in with his steel clipboard and a pencil hanging from it by a string. This reminded her that, earlier that day, she'd met a friend for lunch at a Chinese restaurant, and her waiter had a pencil tied to his notepad. As she'd cracked open her fortune cookie, a toddler grabbed the waiter's pencil and yanked the notepad from his hand, causing a scene. Her fortune read, 'A big break is coming.'

"My father stood in the doorway that night, years of sadness in his eyes, and said one thing: 'I need a break.' As he said that word — *break, rotura* — the phone started ringing, and the dog next door barked. I know all this to be true. A delivery man was bringing Chinese food up to the house next door and — my mother could not believe it — the delivery man was an ex-boyfriend of hers from long ago. She recognized his face crystal clear in her mind from decades before.

"Then the answering machine picked up the call. It was her boss from the yoga studio saying that he needed to let her go. He told her the date of her last class, which happened to be the date of her and my father's anniversary.

"With tears running down her face as all these separate threads intersected in the span of seconds, she remembered that her father had left her mother in the same way, with a similarly simple declaration from the front door upon returning home from work one day.

"It was right then that I walked into the kitchen. I was ten, and in my hands I held the two pieces of a porcelain statue from her dresser, an elegant Chinese dancer. Oblivious to everything that had just happened, I said, 'No quise romperlo'—'I didn't mean for it to break.' And at this last word, I saw, in my mother's eyes—I tell you, Elliot, I saw this—her soul shattered like a mirror. Never was she the same. Never." Her eyes were glassy now. "Still she lives in the institution."

I stared at my half-eaten chicken, silent. Was I to take it, then, that she assumed her mother's tragic string of coincidences meant an organizing power had to exist, and she was using the power of the stars, this Triple Alpha Reaction, to harness it? That there could be no other explanation? Or was she delusional, grasping for a rational underpinning to a giant cosmic fluke? Or, worse (or perhaps more probable), was her mother just flat-out insane, and the apple didn't fall far from the tree?

As my lips worked out which of these avenues to pursue, I couldn't help but overhear a conversation from the next table. "Yeah, my sister just got a divorce," the man said. "She moved in with me. She's driving me nuts. Used to be some big musician. Now all her health food's crowding up the refrigerator."

I whipped around. "Hey, what's the big idea?" I snapped. The looks from their table were ugly and dismissive.

"What the hell is this?" I shot at the doctor. "Did you set me up? You talk to Mercer about me, or Eccleson? One of your research grunts make a file on me? Did Benny tell you *Terminator 2* was my favourite movie? That I like Chicken Parmigiana?" My hand gripped the white tablecloth. I could've ripped it off.

But the doctor's face, improbably, looked on me with an adoration I found infuriating. "Oh no, Elliot. Never. It just—it works, you see?" Her excitement drew attention from other tables. "Oh my God, it works."

"Let me show you," she kept anxiously saying on the car ride back. "Let me show you."

My tongue stayed stuck in my cheek. It was looking for a rational explanation or an escape from embarrassment.

As we drove up to the R Building, I asked her one more time. "You're honestly telling me that wasn't just a coincidence at the restaurant. Some guy right behind me in the exact same life situation as me."

Her eyes were soft. "I know this makes no sense."

"Someone references a song I haven't heard in years, and later that day I hear that song on the radio. That coincidence is evidence of—what? Some underlying cosmic force? Or my delusional desire for meaning in an empty universe? Isn't it just my mind finding meaning between two separate events so as not to feel so damn alone?"

Her nod was thoughtful and deep. Then she pointed toward the building.

I followed. In the warehouse, she clapped above her head and declared, "We need a circle, please!" Research assistants from every corner converged on us. The alien-looking contraption in the corner—a humming steel ball of wires and tubes, both haphazard and elegant in its design—hummed a low reverberation I felt in my tailbone.

The assistants formed a circle. Nearly twenty of them, plus me. The doctor pointed, and one said, "Uh, my middle name is Andrew."

"That's my middle name," I said, disbelieving.

"We went to grade school together." Another pointed back and forth between me and her. "I remember sitting by you in Mrs. Durkin's class in fourth grade."

"My birthday is June tenth," someone said.

"Mine too."

"My mom's."

"My cat's."

People continued. Two had walked down the aisle to the same obscure Velvet Underground song. Three had fathers who were cruise directors. Two had broken bathroom mirrors this month. Four had irrational fears of cacti, eliciting much laughter.

Then someone said, "I obsessively hunt for obscure DVDs of TV shows."

"Oh my God, no you don't," I cried out.

"I do too. Nineties sitcoms. English and British. Mostly mint condition. What do you collect?"

My eyes searched for Dr Jimenez. Her rooted gaze was expecting my look. "Look beyond cause and effect, Elliot. It's just the connection, the connection that was always there. Just the eight of diamonds finding itself over and over. What I need is helium, power, and equipment. Now you know what this is. So you tell me: what should I write in these budget transfer rationales?"

My tongue was hanging out of my mouth. I'd barely heard her question. "But we were all put here, on paths to this moment, long before the machine was built."

"Humans experience time in the linear," she lectured. "But the fabric of the universe itself is woven from forces beyond our comprehension."

All nodded. But I found my own head shaking. "If Upstairs discovers this … If people find out what you've done …"

"Oh, they will, Elliot. And we'll be ready." She crossed her arms and her eyes grew wide and defiant. "Eventually the connection will be made. In the end, all connections are made."

"But ..." My mind reeled. "My social security number?" I explained RP 916-00-3871 to everyone, too excited to care that I was giving away my most sensitive piece of personal information. "The number was assigned prior to the project, prior to the reaction, prior to—"

"That—" She pointed at me, then at everyone, enjoying every second. "*That* is coincidence."

Her staff had seemed to fan around her now, all staring at me. In that moment, the warehouse stood silent but for the machine humming in the background, churning on.

916-00-3871

Mercer texted me that Saturday morning while Kelsey and I were at the farmers' market. I couldn't believe she got me to go with her. Apparently I'd get to eat what she cooked. I told her I'd buy an apple or something.

Auditors coming Monday, his text read. *Should debrief beforehand bc I was out those two days this week.* Why was Mercer out Thursday and Friday? He'd sprained his ankle falling off a ladder. Getting something down from a cabinet for his mother. In the kitchen.

I'll be there if you want, I wrote, *but I'd just read the budget rationales. What about Eccleson?* Grizzled, disillusioned vets were usually good at that kind of thing.

Actually, Eccleson took next week off. Had a come-to-Jesus moment after he fell off a ladder and sprained his ankle real bad. Unbelievable, right???

And then, *What does this mean: For helium purchases needed for research into Occurriential Interdeterminism utilizing Triple Alpha Reaction???*

Go visit Dr Jimenez, I texted. *Building R.*

"Put that thing away." Kelsey's voice pulled me back to the farmers' market, the booths and the people in the sunshine, the colourful peppers and tomatoes and leafy greens. "You're walking around like Tommy. Deaf, dumb, and blind."

I froze a second. "Wow. Reaching for that reference."

Around we walked, taking in the smells of fresh flowers, the arrays of squash, cabbage, tomatoes, carrots, spice jars, cheeses, fresh bread. I bought a small bumpy red fruit that I had never seen before.

"You have no intention of eating that."

I agreed. I had no idea what it was. It just looked cool.

In one corner of the market, a bunch of bearded men sat in a circle of folding chairs with guitars and ukuleles. We stood amongst the crowd, and when one song ended another began that we both recognized but, looking at each other, couldn't place. It hit us both at the same time: 'Pinball Wizard'.

"No way," she said.

"They were inspired by your insult," I said. She pushed me.

Right into someone. I apologized profusely to the man, who just laughed it off. An older guy, curly grey beard, Hawaiian shirt, sunglasses. "No worries, man, no worries. But you can make it up to me. Come check out my wares. Got a mini garage sale in my trunk over there." He pointed just beyond the fence to a wood-panelled station wagon. "You a musician?" He pointed at Kelsey. "I can see by the way you move your mouth to the music. Got something for you."

Kelsey shrugged, so we followed him around the fence. As his head bobbed, he said, "Name's Dr Jimenez. Specialize in curiosity." And he opened the trunk.

Boxes of clothes, trinkets, records. But nothing that looked like crap. "You a violinist? No, not with them fingers … here I gotchu, I gotchu."

As he pulled something out for Kelsey, I was going through boxes. VHSs. Video games. And yes, DVDs. My fingers flipped as fast as they could. I had a feeling.

And there, improbably, buried in an old box of B-movies, was the complete series of *Nero Wolfe*, the TV show I'd been trying to track down for months.

Notes emerged from behind me. The man had given Kelsey a flute, and now, for the first time since the divorce, she was playing something. Took me a minute to recognize it. Then there it was. 'Pinball Wizard'.

My hand grabbed frantically at the first *Nero Wolfe* DVD case, but before my thumbs pried it open they hesitated, feeling the black plastic, wondering what would be inside.

THE HUMMINGBIRD FLASH FICTION PRIZE

THE 2021 HUMMINGBIRD FLASH FICTION PRIZE

Ornate and bold, hummingbirds effortlessly capture our attention with their equally graceful and daring manoeuvres. This year's finalists certainly captured our attention and introduced us to colourful characters and landscapes.

Bob Thurber, master of flash fiction, joined us once again in the judge's seat, and we are delighted to share with you the winners of the 2021 Hummingbird Flash Fiction Prize. Bob described the winning story, 'The Art of Ironing', which appears in this issue, as "A neat portrait packed full of colourful descriptions and vivid imagery." Honourable mentions will appear in subsequent issues of *Pulp Literature*.

FIRST PLACE: 'The Art of Ironing' by **Natalie Harris-Spencer**

RUNNER-UP: 'Out in the Sticks' by **Kevin Sandefur**

HONOURABLE MENTIONS: 'Clothesline' by **Kimberley Aslett**; 'The Realm of Shadows' by **Megan W Shaw**

Bob called the shortlist "a meritorious batch of stories, each of them with obvious merit, all requiring careful study. . . . Congratulations to all the writers, and thank you for some enjoyable reads." Congratulations to all the shortlisted authors:

Alex Reece Abbott
Kimberley Aslett

Shanda Connolly
Hannah van Didden
Natalie Harris-Spencer (with two stories)
Maria Marchese
Kevin Sandefur
Megan W Shaw
PG Streeter

A warm thank-you to Bob Thurber for once again lending us his expert judgement and comments, and congratulations to this year's winners.

Natalie Harris-Spencer is an English writer, digital editor, and blogger living in America. Her work has appeared in the Archipelago Fiction Anthology, CultureCult, The Dark City, The Satirist, The Stonecoast Review, *and more. She was selected by* Oyster River Pages *as one of their Emerging Fiction Voices, and she is the winner of the 2021 Hummingbird Flash Fiction Prize. She earned her MFA in Creative Writing at Stonecoast, and she is the Editor-in-Chief of* Aspiring Author. *She is currently working on her second novel. Natalie enjoys surprise in fiction. And tea.*

Kevin Sandefur currently works as Capital Projects Accountant for the Champaign Unit 4 School District. His stories have appeared (or are forthcoming) in The Gateway Review, The Saturday Evening Post, Sunlight Press, Bethlehem Writers Roundtable, *and the Bath Flash Fiction anthology* Restore to Factory Settings. *He lives with his wife and two cats in Champaign County, Illinois, which is a magical place where miracles happen almost every day and hardly anyone seems to find that remarkable.*

The Art of Ironing

by Natalie Harris-Spencer

Some flat afternoons I can smell the starch from my childhood. It comes to me by accident: the high whiff of linen on the bend of a washing line, the dense threat of rain overhead.

With this smell I'm fourteen again, back in my parents' house, miles and miles away, watching my mother do the ironing. There's a shut glass door between us, behind which exists a green dome terrarium. I peer through the glassy orb at my mother: a distortion. She's a rainforest mirage, her mechanical ironing arm slick-hot and hazy.

My mother irons things that don't need ironing: hankies, socks, sheets. There's no art to what she's doing, this procedural flattening of creases, this daily smushing. I think she must really love the monotony of ironing. You'd have to love something that pointless that much.

Other things need ironing. "I have a pile of ironing," she laments, like the pile is akin to a pile of dirt or a pile of bodies, and she really does: my brother's football shorts, my father's work shirts. She has a way with the limbs, rotating them so it's like the board is wearing them. She wriggles the head between the little buttons, around the waistbands. The iron moans with the work. I'm telling you: it isn't art.

"Mum," I say, eager. "I made up a dance in school. Do you want to see?"

"Later. I have a pile of ironing."

I dance alone in the lounge.

One morning, I sneak the iron for my own dirty purposes. I press my cheek to the board, edging the metal as near to my skull as I dare, an acrid smell spitting from my hair. I lift up, tingling. The straightening hasn't worked too well; the ends fray in mad sprigs and the roots retain their curls. Still, I look a little bit more like her: presentable. I will her to notice, patting at my 'do. But no words of approval come; instead, the persistent hiss of steam.

I hate the iron. I hate its pointless swerve, the erasure. But most of all, I hate how it's a dirty thief, how it hoodwinked my mother, claiming all those afternoons from me before my father got home from work.

"Not now, love. I have a pile of ironing and dinner to make before Dad gets home."

I watch her guide the ship shape, the prow of the metal. I note the occasional crackle of days-old water as it hits the scalding plain. She insists on folding the sheets, creating senseless dents. It's the sheets that get me the most: her (not art) work ruined by the dent of a shoulder or the turn of a knee. I destroy her work as I lash out in my sleep, yellow sweat leaking, cells shedding, blood seeping. I knuckle-rub the muddy stains in secret, the smell like a wet coin. Then I bury them in the wicker basket ahead of the next cycle, almost wishing she finds them, craving the confrontation. I feel sorry for the sheets; they're getting ironed again. My mother has that look about her: a narrowing storm.

One day, my mother burns my favourite skirt that she finds too revealing, lifts its alien silver fabric between pinched fingers, her front teeth clamped over her bottom lip as if to say, "Not my fault; the iron made me do it." The imprint resembles a muddy boot, the strange kick of it. I bite back kiddish tears. I loved that skirt.

When a boy finally lies next to me on those sheets, I think, Yes. That'll teach you. My mother doesn't mention when they go missing. She simply replaces them, a higher thread count, neatly plastic-wrapped in poppers. I shake the corners furiously, an expulsion of invisible bed bugs.

"Mum?"

"Yes, love?"

"What happened to my sheets?" I'm provoking her, we both know it.

"What sheets?"

I can't wait to stain them again, to show her how grown-up I am.

Today, over the phone, I tease my mother with kindness about the ironing, its artlessness, about how she was back then.

"You were obsessed!" I accuse. "Who irons sheets, anyway?" We laugh in unison: one mother to another.

Twenty years later, and it's still easier to tease than tell the truth.

OUT IN THE STICKS

by KEVIN SANDEFUR

The first thing I notice is the heat. I can't remember why I ever thought it was a good idea to live in a desert town. There's no such thing as dry heat when your clothes are drenched in sweat.

The bus stop has a shelter, but the canopy doesn't offer much shade, the Plexiglas just magnifies the sun, and of course there are no trees, not in the desert. There's an old man waiting with me. He's so old that I'm surprised he can walk around without help, but there he is, standing straight and tall and proud, still independent. He's wearing a suit and tie, and I can't imagine how he stands it.

The bus comes around the corner, and the old man asks if this one is ours. I tell him yes, it has to be, because it's the only bus that comes down this street, and it goes all the way out of town, all the way out into the sticks, and that's where I need to go.

The bus stops and the doors open, and I swear I can see the chill spilling down the stairwell. I step up into air-conditioned luxury and pull two quarters from my pocket to drop in the coin box, but the driver points at a sign that says '75 cents'.

Damn, I think, it must have gone up. The old man behind me on the steps taps my shoulder and when I turn, he's holding out an extra quarter. I smile and thank him and drop the quarter in the box on top of its partners. The driver clicks the lever, and I step the rest of the way up into the bus.

It's pretty crowded, but I spot Malcolm about halfway back on the right in a window seat. We make eye contact for just a moment before he turns away and looks out the window. A very large woman is sleeping next to him, so I keep looking around.

There's an open seat by a little girl. I point to it to ask her and she nods, so I sit down. I tell her my name, and she smiles. She's maybe nine or ten, and I can tell that she's been sick because her head is shaved and her eyes are dark and hollow. I ask if her parents are on the bus and she says that they stayed behind for now, but they will all catch up with her later.

I glance at the other passengers and notice that most of them are wearing their Sunday best. Only a handful are dressed for comfort, like me.

The bus makes a couple more stops as we move through the city. A woman gets on with a child and a huge bag that hangs loose like there's nothing in it. There are no babies on the bus today, thank god. The last passenger to board is a young soldier in uniform, but there aren't any seats left, so he takes point at the front of the bus, just behind the yellow line, a sentry standing at attention.

I turn to look back at Malcolm, but he keeps looking away, pretending to be fascinated by something outside the window. I want to tell him that I forgive him, that it wasn't all his fault, and that I still love him, but he clearly doesn't want to talk to me right now.

I don't recognize some of the streets passing outside the windows, and I begin to think maybe I might be on the wrong bus after all. But before I can say anything to the driver, we're on a bridge, crossing a dry, concrete riverbed that I've never seen before. The first thing on the other side is a dog park overlooking the empty river, but there's only one guy there, an old man with three mutts on a leash.

After that it's all golf courses and country clubs, boutique malls and churches, and ranch-style stucco houses with mission-tile roofs and irrigated lawns. I wonder how much farther we still have to go, but we keep driving on as the boutiques give way to strip malls and liquor stores and fast food drive-throughs. The houses get smaller as the streets get narrower and more uneven, and there's no more grass, so the yards are just giant litter boxes with the occasional boulder or glass globe or bathtub Madonna.

At last I know we've come to the end of the line because the bus pulls into a parking lot and stops. Through the window I can see the terminal, all glass and chrome and flat against the horizon, but there's nothing else out here: no rocks, no grass, no trees or bushes, not even any sticks.

The driver opens the door, and we can feel the desert air rushing into the bus, much hotter even than it was in the city. We all file out, and the heat is a giant hand pressing the passengers into the pavement like hamburger patties on a diner grill, squeezing the fat and sweat and life out of us.

We try to stagger forward, but the desert sun forces us to squint against the light and the heat squashes us all down as we crawl blindly on our bellies like mole rats melting across the asphalt, hoping that we are heading towards the terminal, and I realize that maybe I do blame Malcolm, just a little bit.

SAP AND SEED

H Pueyo & Dante Luiz

H Pueyo and **Dante Luiz** are a creative duo and couple from southern Brazil. She's a writer of speculative and literary fiction, and her work has appeared in several venues, such as the Magazine of Fantasy & Science Fiction, Clarkesworld, Fireside, and The Year's Best Dark Fantasy and Horror. He's an illustrator, art director for Strange Horizons and Mafagafo Revista, the interior artist of Crema, and an occasional writer of short fiction and non-fiction. 'Sap & Seed' was originally published by Wayward Kindred, an anthology focused on monstrous families. You can find them on Twitter as @dntlz and @hachepueyo.

Sap.

How long until we reach the end of the forest?

I'm hungry...

We have been walking ever since.

Eat from my arm.

Whenever I was hungry, honeydew dripped from his arms.

If it hurt, Sap never told me.

Keep eating and stop bothering me now.
Why do you need to be so frail?
Whining all the time...
Complaining all the time...
When we find another forest, I'll finally be rid of you.
Sap...
Why are you...?

Sap dried up like our mother, like our forest, like everything I knew.

ALLAIGNA'S SONG: CHORALE

JM Landels

JM Landels *is torn between travelling the world to teach writing and swordfighting, and never leaving her idyllic farm in Langley, BC. Her debut series, fantasy bestseller* Allaigna's Song: Overture, *and the sequel,* Aria, *are available from Pulp Literature Press and Amazon. The third book,* Chorale, *is due out soon. You can follow her adventures with pen and sword at jmlandels.stiffbunnies.com. In this issue we present the first part of the final novel in the Allaigna's Song trilogy,* Chorale.

Previously in *Allaigna's Song* . . .

At the end of Allaigna's Song: Aria, *our heroine gave up on the search for her birth father and enlisted in the Brandishear Rangers. Six years later, Allaigna mustered out and accepted a private commission from her grandfather, which took her and a handful of mercenaries, including her cousin Goff, to the wilds of Oburakor, tasked with exploring the ancient arcane Lothgates, long thought to be inactive. After witnessing the cataclysmic destruction of a gate, Allaigna and her companions travel through hostile territory and mountain passes to make it back to the Ilmar, but not without cost.*

VERSE I

DEATH SONG

20 Tarcia 1604

It was Rennielle and I who washed and dressed Goffree's body, after the four of us who remained took turns in pairs carrying him down the mountain pass. We had buried Olenbry in a makeshift cairn of stones and snow in Oburakor. It pained me that we could not bring her body with us, and now Goff would not make it home either. We were back in the Ilmar at least, but far to the north, in a mining town set low against the mountains of eastern Holc. He would not lie beside the heroes of Brandishear, where his heart belonged.

His ribs stood out in the pale winter light of the candleless room. We were all thinner than when we had met, but the lack of warm blood beneath his skin made him seem as if he had been a corpse for longer than these two awful days. As I sponged the dirt and blood of Oburakor from his body, I ran an inventory of his scars: the jagged tear on his calf he had earned in his first days as a squire; the whitened pucker above his clavicle from an Ilvani arrow; countless small and large lines criss-crossing his arms and legs, some old and some far too new; and of course, the one I'd given him, shallow but long, from left shoulder to right hip, so many years ago.

Rennielle watched me run my fingers along it, her sharp, pale brows sunk in a deeper frown than usual. Was she jealous still?

"What do you suppose that is from?" she asked.

I was taken aback. They'd shared a bed, these two. How had she not seen it, not asked him?

"Did he never tell you?"

Her eyes narrowed. "He would not say."

"It was me," I answered, memories clogging my throat with more sadness, wishing that thoughtless act had not robbed us of eight years of friendship. I didn't elaborate. *Let her ask.*

But she said nothing, only continued her meticulous job of washing the left side of his body.

When we had dressed and arrayed him, I took my father's knife and removed two locks of his hair: one for her, and one for me to carry back to Rheran, along with the ashes from the fire we would build that night.

Never had a death song been so hard to pry from my unwilling throat. Later Imerian told me it had been beautiful, sad and soaring, and had done justice to his life. To me it felt like breathing sand.

We stood by the blazing bonfire, the four of us and a handful of villagers who came to pay respects and share the cask of ale we bought. Rennielle stood next to me, both of us scorching from the heat of the blaze yet neither willing to step backward.

At last the villagers melted away into the evening, clutching tankards of ale and murmuring regrets at the loss of such a fine young man. Harthor and Imerian retreated also, leaving the two of us alone by the dimming pyre.

"Your blood blade," Rennielle said in a low voice. "Where did you get it?"

I blinked, startled out of my grief. I was too raw to dissemble. "It was my father's."

"I doubt that," she murmured.

I rounded on her. "Yes, I know you purebred Ilvani can't conceive of mingling your blood with Ilmari. But accept it, princess, it happens."

Her head jerked back as if I had slapped her.

She stepped between me and the fire, her face invisible in the shadow.

"Who said I was a princess?"

The word had been an offhand jibe at her pride and aloofness. I had no idea it would hit so close to the mark. If I had been less wounded, less drained with grief, I would have pursued the comment, delving to discover her secrets.

Instead I stepped away from the fire. My eyes were dry now from the heat, and my face stiff with evaporated tears, as I went in search of Harthor and Imerian.

*L*AURESA'S CHORUS

11—15 Ranis 1598

For three nights straight the dagger has entered Lauresa's dreams. It is her daughter she wants to see, whom she rushes to first amid the cloying confusion of dream shapes, catching a glimpse here or there of her sharp chin and sharper eyes behind the veil of crow's-wing hair, or the curve of her back outlined in the window, the step of her feet on the floorboards, the nimble shadow of her hand as she pares an apple. But each time, the blue watered steel of the blade and the strange carvings of the dagger's hilt thread their way between her and her daughter, bright and blinding, or dark and obscure, with the taste of fear and the smell of threat.

She wakes, and hugs Vardry to her, disturbing the toddler's rest so she can soothe both him and herself by crooning and rocking him back to sleep.

On the fourth morning after Allaigna's departure, Lauresa, more gaunt and worn even than when the twins were newborn, visits her mother and asks her for a sleeping draught.

Irdaign eyes her daughter, her own face as drawn as Lauresa's, but asks no questions.

After the initial tears of desperation and recrimination, after the few rangers stationed at Teillai have been sent out to comb the roads, forests, and countryside, Lauresa allows herself to return to her chamber. It is quiet and cold in the early spring evening, the fire not yet lit and the beds still unmade, for she ushered her children from the room that morning and allowed no maids in all day.

From the false bottom of the footlocker she takes the velvet cloth that has kept the sheathless dagger for all these years. It smells of oil, metal, and, she imagines, him. She has nothing of him now — neither the dagger nor his daughter — but the loss of him is tiny and irrelevant, almost welcome in contrast to the gaping hole in her heart.

Why did she show it to her, she asks herself.

Because Allaigna deserved to know. Because she wanted to show her daughter some proof of her father other than what she could see in her face: the straight dark hair, the pale grey eyes, the sharp chin.

The dagger is irrelevant, she repeats to herself. It is what it represents: the years of lies, of denying Allaigna the most basic of truths about who she is — that has severed the frayed bond between them more cleanly than the sharpest knife. And sent her too-young daughter fleeing into the world.

Too young, too young. The words keep echoing through her head like the refrain of a song.

She wants to blame her mother, who must have foreseen this and failed to prevent it. And yet that anger is tempered with guilt — for Irdaign did far more to prepare Allaigna to survive on her own than Lauresa ever has. Irdaign insisted on weapons masters and tutelage, while Lauresa — all Lauresa ever did for her daughter was try to keep her close and hidden: from the Duke, from the world, and from her fate.

The day Lauresa parted from him fifteen years ago comes back to her.

Teillai's castle rose on the horizon, grey stone against sharp blue winter sky. They slowed their horses from their brisk, travelling trot to a walk.

"Is that it?" asked Lauresa. She couldn't voice the rest of the question: *My new home?*

Einavar—she still prefers that name to his true one—nodded, his eyes unreadable in the shadow of his hood.

"I'll ride with you till we are in sight of the gates." He reached across, caught her hand, his touch sending warmth into her cold fingers, even through the gloves. "Though I wish you'd let me escort you all the way."

The winter wind stung her eyes and nose, making them water. Even Einavar's pale skin was reddened by the cold.

"We've been through this. You know you must be long gone by the time I am recognized and my story told. I'll keep to my lies, and you keep to yours." Her heart complained within her chest, threatening to break free of her ribs. "For all our sakes."

Their horses had stopped, and Lauresa allowed Peri's reins to drop onto the mare's neck, unwilling to let go of Einavar's hand just yet. She reached across herself with her free hand and pulled his dagger from her belt.

"I won't need this any longer." She proffered it, hilt first.

He put his hand on it, enclosing hers, and stared at the blade.

"You do know what it is?"

"An Ilvani blood blade."

"They are forged for one purpose only, and that purpose is usually vengeance." He looked back at her. "This one has been used already. It was the blade Caradar Halobrelia used to carve his sign into your grandfather's corpse at the battle of Welbirk."

She shuddered and pulled back, the sharp back curve of the blade scratching her finger.

"There are many amongst the Valnirati who would dearly love to have this trophy back," he added.

"Where did you get it?" she whispered, her cloudy memory fighting to clear.

"I stole it. From your father's chamber."

"Does he know?"

He shook his head. "It was meant to be put on display—an incitement to move against the Valnirati once more. There are those of us who want neither side to have it.

"I think," he said, his eyes distant, "I will need to rejoin Chanist's service. And it would be best not to have it with me. Keep it hidden, and make sure it never comes to light again."

She nodded, tucked it into her saddlebag, and urged Peri onward to the inevitable point at which she and Einavar would say goodbye.

Verse 2

Family

21–24 Tarcia 1604

There was some argument about where to go, now that we were in friendly territory. Rennielle and Imerian wished to head south directly, crossing into Aerach through the foothills. Harthor, however, was keen to take ship back to Elalantar and wanted the nearest port.

For myself, I had not been to Aerach for at least a half dozen years, and though my heart now felt its call more strongly than ever, I was wary. Wary of renewing an attachment to home and worried, perhaps, that it would turn out I had none.

"And what of our …" I hesitated to use the word 'contract', for I had never made one and was still unsure what deals these other three had struck with Goff or his masters. "Our task? Shouldn't we finish the job?"

Harthor snorted. "It is finished. The lothgate is destroyed, and no armies will be using that pass again."

Our eyes drifted up to the mountains behind the village. No one managed to say out loud that our mission had died with Goff.

"But we have information," I began slowly. "Numbers, maps." I nodded at the map tube Harthor now carried. "Diagrams … and knowledge. Where do we go with that?"

Harthor's face was shuttered. "Our debt to Chanist of Brandishear is paid and more. We owe him nothing."

"What of the people who live here?" I asked.

"We owe them even less," said Rennielle.

"With Essaruk armies gathering on the other side of that range? Our consciences, at the very least, owe them some warning." I locked her strange amethyst eyes with mine. She had a conscience, that much I knew, but would it wake on my call?

"Allaigna is right," came Imerian's soft diplomat's voice. "War is good for none, least of all those who lie in its path. But is it enough to simply pass on our knowledge?"

"No," I said, as the realization hit me. "All the Ilmar needs to know. All the princes. But also the people."

The three of them looked at me, puzzled.

"Harthor, this map shows lothgates all over the Ilmar. And we know Brandishear has been at work opening them. What do you think will happen if they succeed?"

Rennielle's face darkened. "Chanist Brandis will have a stranglehold over all the nations."

I nodded, feeling the force of her hatred toward my grandfather. None of them knew my relationship to him, and it seemed more than ever that my identity was a liability.

"Nonetheless, he needs this knowledge as well." I stopped her protest with a dark look of my own. "Brandishear has been aware of the threat from Oburakor before now. It is undoubtedly the best prepared to deal with it."

I took a breath, feeling the fates shift and slip into place, almost as if I had my grandmother's Sight.

"I will take word to Brandishear. Imerian can carry it to Aerach, and Harthor to Elalantar."

The two men nodded, their looks thoughtful.

"And what of the Ilvani?" I asked Rennielle. "Will your people stand neutral or defend against Oburakor?"

She spread her long fingers, a deflecting gesture. "I cannot answer for my people."

"But you will carry word back?"

She looked away. "I cannot."

I sighed, frustrated at the deliberate vagueness of the woman. And yet, we all had our secrets.

"If that is indeed your father's dagger, you could carry the message yourself," she said.

I took a slow breath. Was that a clue, at last, to the identity of my father? I had given up that search when I enlisted. The thought of renewing it was painful … and enticing.

"I do not know my father." My voice was level, though my heart was racing. "Do you?"

She gave me an even look in return. "No. But the Ilvan high council would. And might tell you. If they did not kill you on sight for soiling a blood blade with Ilmari hands."

Imerian intervened. "We are all forgetting one prince," he said, "and that is the one closest at hand. We can all take word to Adamiel at Sandria, and find our paths from there."

It was two days on foot through the damp and chilly forests and foothills of eastern Holc before we found a settlement with enough horses to sell us. They were surprisingly good ones. None of my companions were as comfortable in the saddle as I, and I chose for them sturdy and even-tempered mounts. But my heart was lost to a leggy black mare, as like in size and colour to my beloved Nag as any I had yet found, though finer boned and hotter tempered. My good sense told me she would be a flighty liability in the rough and spooky terrain we travelled, but she was already mine at first sight. I named her Rhi, after the south wind.

Having a horse beneath me again lifted the heavy sadness that had settled on me, and it helped me forget, from time to time, the lock of Goff's hair and the jar of ashes from his pyre that rested in the bottom of my pack. I came to the gates of Sandria with a song bubbling from my lips and cheer ill-matched to the welcome we received.

Though it was only midday, the gates were barred and held by a pair of soldiers.

"Papers?" asked the nearest.

I opened my mouth to sing a charm that would help him forget the need to vet us, but the song died on my lips. Standing in the shadow of the gate's buttress was a dark-garbed knight. Even without seeing the blazon on his black leather pauldrons and gorget, or his featureless black surcoat, his aura gave him away as one of the Mageguard.

I let the continual song within my chest die, fade, run out through my feet and dissipate in the air. My years in the service of Brandishear had taught me how to hide my magic in this way, and I hoped it was enough to let the Mageguard's notice slide over me. Would he stop Harthor or Imerian, though?

I smiled down at the guard as my new mare danced beneath me.

"Papers? What papers do you mean, good sir?"

He stepped closer, putting a hand on my horse's bridle. The mage had removed himself from the shadow and was strolling nearer.

The guard with the hand on my rein looked familiar as his face turned to mine. I shook my head, blinked to clear the vision, and our words came out at the same time.

"Allaigna?"

"Darras?"

He looked over his shoulder at his companion guard and the mage who still moved in.

"Show me something—anything!" he hissed.

Harthor, quicker of thought than I, produced some folded note papers from his pack.

Darras opened them, frowned at the contents, but snapped it shut and passed it back.

"Thank you—on you go," he said loudly, and waved to the tower to have the portcullis lifted.

To me, so quietly I could barely hear it, he said, "Nag's Head," as I passed by him, dumbfounded.

I avoided eye contact with the Mageguard as we pushed into the walled city of Sandria. It was only as the portcullis dropped behind us that I realized Darras had referred not to my horse's anatomy, but to an inn.

We chose a different inn to stable our horses and take rooms. It was not that I mistrusted Darras, but the unaccountable presence of my foster brother as a city guard, in Holc of all places, was too much of a surprise to leave me entirely at ease. That, and the disturbing locked-down aspect of the city itself, had put my nerves on alert. Harthor and Imerian argued against my decision to meet Darras alone, but I had far too many personal questions to ask, and I refused their company. At last I agreed they could come to the Nag's Head and sit far away, though it was still more scrutiny than I wanted when meeting my brother for the first time in six years.

The evenlamps had come on when I opened the door of the inn. A glance across the room showed Imerian and Harthor already ensconced in a corner with a jug of ale. Darras's shock of wheat-straw hair was nowhere to be seen, so I ordered a flagon of watered wine and took myself to a table by the smoke-darkened windows to watch the door.

He must have come from an upstairs room, for I was surprised by a touch on my shoulder. I twisted on the bench, made to get up, but he stopped me, his hand holding me to my seat by the shoulder while the other brought my fingers to his lips for a brief kiss.

"No family reunion, here, Allaigna," he said, moving around the table to seat himself across from me without letting go my hand. "There are eyes everywhere, and I'd rather they saw you as a pretty girl on whom I have intentions, than as my sister."

"Darras ..." So many questions bounced inside my head, fighting to see which would escape my mouth first. I started with the obvious. "What are you doing here?"

He used my hand to draw us closer across the table. "I might ask you the same. But not here."

He glanced at Harthor and Imerian. "Will your minders object if we remove to my room?"

I smiled, amused at the thought. I had told them I knew Darras, but no more than that. Let them think what they would.

"No doubt," I replied, my smile turning mischievous as I stood.

I drew Darras up with me, and linked my arm in his as we left the room, winking at Imerian over my shoulder.

It was good to be in Darras's presence again. He had always looked up to me with a mixture of little-brother admiration and, though I didn't see it at the time, puppy love. The fact he was clearly glad to see me warmed me.

He closed the door behind us and wrapped me in his arms: a man's arms, not those of the gangly thirteen-year-old I'd left behind in Teillai. For the first time in my life I realized how good-looking he was. The world was unsteady beneath my feet. Darras was not the foster brother I remembered. Life had changed him as much as it must have changed me, and I no longer knew who I was or who I wanted to be.

The embrace didn't last long. He stepped back, still holding me by the shoulders.

"Fingal's teeth, Allaigna, but it's good to see you. Where have you been?"

He was shaking, his face a mix of relief, joy, and worry. I pulled back further, taking him in. Not just his new and handsome height, but the hardened muscles under his shirtsleeves and the puckered scar beneath his left ear, still pink and new.

I grasped his forearms, squeezed, and felt my own knees start to shake. "It's a story so long I don't know where to start." I looked around the small room. There were no chairs, only a bed. "Can we sit?"

In the end I told a much shorter story than I could have. My inborn reticence, even in front of family, curbed the tale that might otherwise have unfolded. For family he was, if not by blood, and it was family I had run from and still not returned to. Six years in the Brandishear Rangers is what he learned. Nothing of the death of my betrothed, or the path I'd taken to get there. Nothing of this last mission. I also neglected to tell him I was no longer in Brandishear's service. His eyes were troubled throughout, and I sensed a chill settling in the air between us as I talked.

"No word in six years," he said at last. "We feared you dead, Allaigna."

I raised an eyebrow. "And Angeley? Did she think me dead too?"

He shook his head, a slight smile on his lips. "She never doubted you were somehow alive. At least not to us. Privately though … it aged her, Allaigna. You leaving us."

Guilt such as I'd never yet felt washed through me. I distracted myself with another thought. When, I mused, had Darras become so perceptive?

"How is she?" I asked. "And Mother?"

He spent till the next bell talking of home, of Mama and Angeley, of Allenry, my sisters, and little Vardry, whom I hardly knew at all. When I searched for it, I found my anger at them gone, and nothing there but a deep well of tears that rose beyond my capacity to hold them back. We sat for a long time, his brotherly arm around me and our backs to the crumbly plaster of the wall, while six years of sadness I didn't know I had within me made itself known.

At last, empty and vulnerable, I wiped my eyes on my sleeve and laughed a little. "But enough of my wallowing, little brother. Tell me of you. How is it you're working as a city guard in Sandria, of all places?"

I twisted to look at him, worried suddenly at how he could have fallen from the path of knighthood. His normally open expression became shuttered, and I knew what he told me was only the official story.

"An affair of the heart led me here. A troupe of dancers came through Osthegn, and I followed them … and her … to Sandria."

It might make a good tale for casual acquaintances, but I didn't believe a word of it.

"It was Lauriana, wasn't it?" I said, caught by a sudden flash of intuition, the faintest echo of my grandmother's talent. "Father chased you off." It felt strange to call Duke Andreg 'Father' after all these years of searching fruitlessly for my real one.

Darras caught the hesitation in my voice and took it for emotion of another sort.

"I caused her no dishonour, Allaigna, I swear it."

I smiled in an attempt to reassure him, though I had a hard time picturing the boy I'd last known tempting anyone into dishonour. "But still," I scolded gently, "she's but fifteen, and you a grown man." That was a bit of flattery, I'll admit. Grown, yes, and nearly a man, but now I could see the boy in those eighteen-year-old eyes.

He was deadly serious, though. "Fifteen is near time for her to be married. I told you, Allaigna, I caused her no dishonour. Merely objected to her betrothal."

"To whom?" I asked, remembering why I'd left home, and the fate of my own betrothed.

"Vallieri."

I sat bolt upright, turning to face him. "Prince Vallieri? Vishod's heir? But he's in his forties. And married."

"A widower," Darras corrected. "For the second time." I could see the pain in his eyes, and the feelings he had for Lauriana that were more than a brother's concern. "For what it is worth, Allenry protested as well."

"And?"

"And what? Your father will hardly disinherit him. He continues his advance through the ranks of court. He's Varanry's squire now."

Varanry was Vishod's second son, next in line to the throne of Aerach after Vallieri.

"But you …"

"Shipped off to Holc."

"As a man-at-arms? Not even a squire? What did your father have to say?"

"Whatever he might have had to say, he is Andreg's vassal. The Duke wants me far away from your sister." There was less bitterness in his voice than I might have expected. "But I chose not to be squired here."

That surprised me. Darras had planned his life's track straight and easy: page, then squire, then landed knight and heir to his father's holdings in southern Aerach. But no, something was not right. I looked him in the eye, allowing my sight to blur and asking the truth to make itself clear instead. But I had not my grandmother's talent. All I could see was that he was lying.

Irdaign's Chorus

Lirrith 1598

Late in the month of Lirrith, Morran Rhoan walks into my garden, unannounced and road-weary. I stand, brushing the soil from my apron and greet him with contained surprise. I had expected a letter, not a personal visit.

"Morran," I breathe, struck as always by his handsome gallantry as he kisses my hand.

"I am so sorry, my lady," he says.

"Just Angeley, here," I interrupt, allowing the correction to mask my concern. "Sorry for ...?" I can barely ask through the anxiety clogging my throat. My rational brain knows the Sight would have warned me if anything dire had happened to Allaigna, but the appearance of the man who has been her guardian these past months sends all my fears alight once more. "Where is she?"

"I put her in the care of your people — saw her safe with the caravan at Cadaurwen."

"But?"

"She left them. Went to Rheran on her own, and apparently" — his brow creases, and I can see in that moment he genuinely cares for her — "she signed on. With the Sixth Rangers at the press ..."

I sigh, feel the wheels and blocks of fate tumble into position. I tried, but this one of three paths I've seen has won out. I don't know if it will make her eventual task easier or harder, but I know it is the road with most peril along the way. Nonetheless, the gelling of destinies lifts a weight from my mind — one that has oppressed me since she left four months ago.

"Thank you." I kiss him on both cheeks. "You have done me, and the Ilmar, a greater service than you know. Will you come in and take refreshment?"

He nods, puzzled by my lack of ire. "I will, but ... I've left my horse in the courtyard." And here he blushes like a fourteen-year-old. "With Captain Rhiadne."

I feel the smile break through my body like sun through thunderheads. My Sight does not give me the pleasure of surprises often, and that this one is happy is a double blessing.

"Well, then, have the grooms look after that and bring her in as well."

I install Rhoan and Rhiadne in the guest chamber, and have food brought to the octagonal room so Lauresa and I can toast the newly betrothed couple. They are en route to Elalantar by ship, where, after nearly two decades apart, they will wed at last.

Rhiadne takes leave of us first, for she has many old friends to see in the castle from her years in Andreg's service. And then Lauresa and I hear from Rhoan, in the beautifully remembered detail of a bard, all that has befallen Allaigna these past months.

We are transfixed: captivated as we share her anguish and her triumphs. The murder of Tiern Doniver shakes my daughter. I have kept that detail I gleaned from the Sight to myself until now. Lauresa has only heard the story the rest of Aerach knew: that Doniver was killed by a mistress.

Rhoan shakes his head. "That weighs heavily on her still. I'm not sure she will ever forgive herself."

"Nor should she," I reply, ignoring the tearful, horrified face of my daughter. "A life taken, even by accident, should never leave one's conscience." I put my hand on Lauresa's. "In the end it will make her stronger—and more cautious."

Lauresa says nothing, though her face is awash in tears and pain. It is not just the generation's distance that allows me to temper my response, or the fact I've known this news for longer. It is that I already know what it is like to feel a daughter's trials, to wish to take that burden on myself, and to be powerless to help.

A week later Lauresa and I bid farewell to Morran and Rhiadne as they ride for the seaport. I know Lauresa, like I, feels the emptiness the couple leaves behind, taking their dual connection to Allaigna with them. Their story in her life is not over, but I wish them some well-deserved years of peace and happiness before they are needed once more.

"She is safe enough," I say to Lauresa, knowing my daughter's thoughts.

"In the Rangers? With border skirmishes growing ever more frequent? And my father angling for war again?"

"We don't know Chanist's thoughts," I reply, though I do know they are unpredictable, and my sources have told me he is back in his cups again. Instead I say, "Chriani is one of the finest captains in the corps. Rhiadne confirms this herself."

She shoots me a venomous look. "I know that, Mother." Her emotions are running so hot she doesn't even check over her shoulder for unwanted ears before addressing me as 'Mother'. "But what soldier is ever safe? No matter how skilled the soldier or the commander?"

"Who among us is ever safe, Lauresa? A fall from a horse could kill one of those two turtle doves"—I gesture to the gate through which our guests have left—"before they ever see Orey."

Or their ship could sink before it reaches port. Your children all could have died a hundred deaths in the nursery, the stable yard, or at the dining table. We have given her all the tools we can, my love. We gave her tutors, and tests of character, and our love. All we can do now is hope and trust."

For a rare moment Lauresa allows herself to be a child again and lets me wrap my arms around her.

"She is strong and clever, and wise beyond her years. You must know that."

She nods into my shoulder.

"Then trust the fates, Lauresa. And trust her."

Dawn comes early at this time of year, and, as usual, I awaken when the sky has just begun to lighten. I lie in bed a few moments, listening to the whisper of barn owls as they return from their night's hunting and the surviving mice that rustle into the safety of the stable walls.

I know I haven't long before the horses begin shuffling in their stalls, pawing at the doors and nickering for breakfast. I want to be gone before Hardin's son Wulf gets up to feed them. But it is so hard to leave the warmth of this bed, the clean smell of horses and hay, and the gently snoring man beside me. I always try to return to my own chamber before the household arises to ask awkward questions.

Careful not to wake him, I brush a lock of Hardin's black and silver hair from his face and steal a kiss of his brow before I edge off the straw mattress and gather my clothes. Not carefully enough, it seems, for his thick forearm encircles my waist and pulls me back.

"Stay," he murmurs into my hip bone, his beard prickling my cold skin.

I roll back around, pinning him to the bed with my weight. "I'd love to."

I kiss him again, this time on the lips: a prim, silencing kiss, with no invitation to linger. "Duty calls."

"Duty? A duty to return to your bed and pretend to have slept there all night?"

"Duty to uphold a semblance of respectability as befits my station. I can't be seen skulking around like a guilty adolescent."

His other arm comes around me, anchoring me to the bed. "Then make it respectable. Marry me."

His tone is casual — playful, even — but there is a gruff edge to his voice and an intensity in his dark eyes, even in this grey half-light, that lets me know he is serious.

I remember another morning almost thirty-five years ago, and another bedroom proposal that changed my life forever. Chanist's face shimmers over Hardin's. The cool light of this early dawn is washed away with the warm sun of that ancient one, and it is I lying on the bed, Chanist's square hard fingers gentle as butterflies as he strokes my belly.

I blink back the past, focus my watery vision on the man before me. "Why would you want an old woman, with fifty-three winters under her feet, as a wife?" I smile to take the sting from my words and ease the hurt they cause me as well. "You're only just past forty, Hardin. A younger woman will last you better."

He reaches up, twines a lock of my hair, as much silver as gold now, between his fingers. "I'm reaching beyond my station, aren't I?" He tries to keep his voice light, but I can feel the wrenching pain waiting to break free. It echoes in my own heart, but the words trouble me.

"A stable master's station is hardly less than a nurse's."

"That might be true if you were only a nurse. But we all know who truly runs Osthegn."

I open my mouth to deny it, but he continues. "But that's not what I meant. A princess might take a groom to bed, but she'd never marry one."

I sit up so suddenly the strand of hair he's been playing with jerks and pulls, bringing tears to my eyes.

"Who told you that?" I whisper, aware of the increased stirring from the horses below and the fact Wulf will soon be up.

"Your daughter," he replies. "You don't think I'd ask for your hand without consulting the head of the household, do you?"

My head is reeling. I'm offended that he would ask anyone's permission, that he had revealed our affair. And to Lauresa no less. And that she would give away this longest-kept secret: that I am her mother, not just her children's nurse.

And worst of all: "And … she gave … you her … blessing?"

He smiles tentatively, his eyes nervous. "She did."

He is right to be wary. There is a volcanic fury in me, ready to erupt. I need to leave this room before that happens.

Despite my molten heart, my smile is fixed with ice.

"How kind of her. But I'm afraid that blessing is not hers to give."

I throw on my clothes and leave, my trembling voice barely able to sing the charm that conceals me from the now-bustling stable yard.

Later that morning, I find Lauresa in her study reviewing the household accounts. She looks up at me, pinching the bridge of her nose between thumb and middle finger, massaging away the stress I see in her tired blue eyes. My maternal instinct nearly catches me off guard, lulling me into sympathy and concern for my daughter, but I will not let this anger go so easily.

I close the door behind me and slip the bolt so as not to be disturbed. With measured steps I cross to Lauresa's desk by the mullioned window, and lean on it, looming over her with a hand on each corner of the table.

"Have you quite lost your senses, daughter?" My voice is soft, but the sudden sharpening in those eyes tells me she senses the danger beneath it.

She sits back in her chair, placing her quill in its inkpot with deliberate slowness, but says nothing.

Her face is no longer beneath mine, so I straighten, our eyes still locked. At first I wonder if she is going to ask me what my complaint is, but there is awareness in that blue gaze. I wait her out.

She breaks the deadlock first, glancing out the window.

"Are you referring to Master Hardin, Mother?"

"You know I am."

She looks back at me, more composed, and I feel my upper hand slipping.

"Then no, I feel my senses are all still where I left them."

The fury inside me starts to bubble its way to the surface, slipping through cracks in my composure.

"Then why," I ask, my voice working hard not to tremble, "after fifteen years of maintaining this secret, have you let it slip? To a stable hand."

There is contempt in my voice at that last phrase, which surprises and grieves me.

Her chin tilts and her eyes sharpen more, pinning me. "A stable hand who loves you, Mother. Though I see now you certainly don't return that affection."

That accusation hits like a kick to the stomach, but I haven't the time now to ask myself whether I truly love Hardin, or simply care for him, or have just been using him to assuage my needs. Instead, I kick back, my rage flowing freely now.

"How dare you, of all people, talk to me of love? You dangle men's affections between your fingers and trail them behind you like cast-off linen. How many of my grandchildren are bastards, Lauresa?"

As soon as the words leave my mouth, I want to reel them back in. I have never, ever maligned my daughter for Allaigna's birth, nor Vardry's, though I only suspect him to be another man's child.

"I'm sorry," I breathe, tears squeezing out of eyes that can no longer face hers. "I'm so sorry, Lauresa. I didn't mean that."

But she is calm, unhurt, or so it seems, by my outburst.

"Yes, you did, Mother. And you know as well as I that the middle four are all Allenis's. If you wanted to know about Vardry, you had only to ask."

I open my eyes and look at her sitting behind her desk, her hands folded calmly across her middle.

There, in her chin and her eyes, I see Chanist, and am moved once more to tears that make me turn away.

"But this isn't about me. How long are you going to let my father stop you from having your own happy ending?"

"This is not about your father either, Lauresa," I reply, struggling to regain control of my voice, my thoughts, the conversation. "You betrayed my trust. For fifteen years, no one in this castle, save you and I, knew who I really am."

"And what should I have told him, Mother, when he came to ask for my nurse's hand? That, no, I wouldn't release you from service?"

"You could have given him leave without telling him who I am."

"So you could break his heart and still leave him in the dark? I knew you'd never tell him. You guard your secrets far too jealously for that. I thought he deserved to know."

I laugh, a dry and humourless sound. "And you think his deserving to know outweighs the risk that this will get back to your husband? And the consequences of that?"

I turn back to her. Her blue eyes have softened, looking more than ever like Chanist's.

"I can't see those consequences like you can. I don't know that they truly exist. I can't live my life playing to some handwritten destiny only you can see. I am tired. So tired of secrets.

"My home, my risk. I chose to tell him because it seemed to be the honourable — the *right* — thing to do."

I am ashamed. And proud of my daughter, who has more courage and integrity than I.

"And," she says, "I want you to be happy. Does your vision show you any happiness left to come with my father?"

I shake my head, half smiling. "The Sight is never so clear as that. Possibilities come into existence and wink out all the time."

"And you are saving yourself for one of these firefly hopes?"

I shake my head again, but she has seen it. I am still saving my hand, if not my body, for that dim and uncertain future I have seen in which we are reunited.

But what I say is, "I am saving myself for my grandchildren. When they are grown and safe, then and only then will I remarry."

I leave the room before she can argue. I am no longer angry, but no closer to a solution as to what to do with my suitor.

There is a dull impatience within me. It is one I have felt before — the sensation of marking time, holding my place in life until events of import unfold. It is not the same as the golden periods: Lauresa's childhood, and my early days here at Teillai before Allaigna left the first time. Those were blissful days of smoothly ticking time, of which I savoured every moment, slowing my heartbeat to not let them pass too fast.

Now, though, I want to push the clock forward, hurry its ponderous ticks that pass like the plodding hooves of a cart horse when I want them to gallop. Is it because all I can do now is wait? Allaigna is gone, her fate beyond all but the most distant touch of my influence. My hands will be required again on the tiller of fate, but for now any action of mine would only serve to steer it off course. Instead I must occupy myself with smaller projects, which is why I have allowed myself the luxury of taking to Hardin's bed. It was rash and foolish. A welcome distraction to be sure, but too large a risk when weighed against the elaborate web of secrecy I have built here. And unfair as well. For I should never have allowed him to give me his heart without being able to offer my hand.

A Leisanmira wedding would do, I mused. Seven years is just about how long I predict this waiting period to last. But he is not Leisanmira, and I can tell without using the Sight it would wound him far too deeply if I were to walk away from him after that time. And if I am honest with myself, I know I, too, would find it even harder. But, most of all, there is the risk that I must be free before seven years are up.

So I will turn him down, and pull apart our hearts while the bonds between them are light and will not bleed too much when broken.

It is even harder than I thought. I bring all my reasons for saying no into the argument: Chanist, Lauresa, my grandchildren, even Tærysh, poor dear Genissa, and Goff, whom I have never met as an adult. I tell myself it is the greater good of the Ilmar that weights my decision, but in all honesty it is my family, and my selfish love for them, that helps me stay the course. I see them, someday, beneath the same roof, and whether that vision is literal or figurative, prophetic or just desperate hope, it holds me up when all I'd rather do is fall into Hardin's arms.

His face is heavy with disappointment, but resigned.

"Aye, I knew as soon as I learned who you were you'd not have me. Even before that, if you must know."

I reach a hand out to comfort, to deny that I would under other circumstances have turned him down, but he continues.

"But I won't stop trying, mind."

My hand stops in mid-air between us. "Won't stop?"

"Aye, lass." That he could call me, a grandmother with more than fifty winters on my bones, 'lass' warms my heart. "I'm not royalty, I know. But it's been a score of years and more since you've had your prince to bed. I'd say he's a lost cause by now."

My eyebrows shoot upward, incredulous at the man's cheek, and my hands land on my hips. I am not about to explain the forces beyond our control that have separated Chanist and me, nor the complexities of politics and fate that keep us apart still.

"It's more complicated than that," I say.

He takes a step nearer. He is a hand or so taller than I, so I have to look up to face him.

"Oh, no doubt," he says. "Far too complicated for a simple mucker like me. I understand ponies, not politics. But I know a thing or two about you as well."

He threads his arms through mine, locking them together. "Like how it was you who kissed me the first time. And invited yourself up here."

He gives a little tug, the tiniest nudge, really, and I fall the half step forward so our bodies touch from hip to chest. Try as

I might to summon the spectre of fate and vision of my family, I can't stop the warmth I feel as my form fits into his.

It is true we resemble our animals. He even looks like Andreg's bay stallion, Challenger, with his wide dark eyes, rich brown skin, and black hair just streaked here and there with grey.

Lost in that animal thought, and the animal betrayal by my body, I barely hear his next words.

"I've had my wife; you've had your husband. If you just need me as your bed mate, I can live with that, Angeley. Or should I call you Irdaign?"

That shakes me awake. "Angeley," I say. "Here and now, I'm Angeley."

"Angeley, then." He pulls me tighter, gives me a kiss as soft and tender as a mother's to her babe.

I sigh, resigned, knowing I will be back in his chamber tonight.

"You'll see," he murmurs into my hair. "I'll make an honest woman of you yet."

1599

As the years have passed, it has become no easier to scry Allaigna. Visions of her life come to me in dreams or unbidden flashes of Sight, but when I make the deliberate effort to view her, the pendant Glaignen gave her, curse him, blocks my sight.

She was without it for a brief window, one I nearly missed since I had been trying fruitlessly for so long. I calculate she lost it somehow between Gleoran and Rheran, but I failed to notice the absence until she had sworn service to Chanist again. Once Allaigna was within the Bastion, the wards there prevented my Sight entirely. But exercises in the field were another matter.

I can see her in my bowl as if I were there, riding out with the Sixth Rangers. She's not riding Nag, I see, but a chestnut Sandbred mare, and I wonder where that came from. She and the mare both seem frail amid the burly men, road-hard women, and thick-cannoned hacks of the Sixth. But I note that her usually pale skin is sun browned, her legs are longer and stronger, and her bare arms show muscles I've never seen before. My eyes fill with love, threatening to erase this long-sought-after vision.

The next day when I try again it is even easier to summon her in my bowl. I am tempted, oh so tempted, to reach out and speak with her, but I fear I might frighten her away. She has made no call to me in all these months, and I won't step in uninvited now.

They camp for the night near the southern border of a forest. It is not the Valnirata, but one of the smaller friendlier woods that still dot Brandishear here and there. The company is relaxed, obviously not fearing any enemy, for they light a fire, sing songs, and tell off-colour jokes that make Allaigna's cheeks turn even redder than the firelight makes them.

Chriani has changed, too, since I last saw him. His hair is military short now, his face tanned and sporting a still-pink scar on the edge of his jaw above the line of a thin beard I hadn't thought he could grow.

The woman who is leading the company in their songs has a fine strong voice with perfect pitch and modulation, of which I approve. She finishes the rousing song, drinks from her canteen, and nestles into Chriani's outstretched arm. They are comfortable together, and quite obviously lovers. I feel a pang of resentment, which I know I have no right to feel. He, too, deserves happiness.

I am loath to leave the vision despite the late hour in Aerach, where the sun sets earlier. I watch and listen well into the night

as each of the company sings a song. I can tell much about them
by their choices and voices, and am comforted by at least the
outward appearance of a good band of comrades for my grand-
daughter. Chriani picks his company well. At last it is Allaigna's
turn, and I expect her to demur, as she would have in so many
similar situations growing up. But most of a year on the road has
made her bold, it seems. She chooses a quiet ballad, not sad, but
slow and sweet to ease the company into the night. The choice
is a good one, and her voice is even finer. I savour each note as it
vibrates out, pure and clear here, rich and throaty there, with a
range and resonance that belies her age and slight build. There
is not a hint of spellsong in it. It is music, pure and simple, and
I can tell it is as hard for her to keep the arcane power out of
her voice as it would be for some to add it in.

I am impressed, awed even, by the talent her audience can't
begin to appreciate.

Chriani, though, seems to see some of it, for he can't take his
eyes off of her, and there is a protective tenderness I am grateful
for in his eye.

I neglect many of my morning tasks, so eager am I to return to
the scrying bowl. Like a woman who has been bereft of food, I
can't help but gorge myself on the sight of her.

The rangers are packing up their gear and saddling their
horses when Chriani's head snaps around and he hisses his
company to silence. Allaigna has heard it too, for her eyes point
down the road with Chriani's.

The band is suddenly alert, swords loosened in scabbards,
while one or two members begin stringing bows. They are not
so far from the Valnirata as I first thought, then, or the figure

coming down the road would not cause this degree of readiness.

His red hair bobs into view first as he climbs the rise in the road, followed by his freckled smiling face.

Chriani calls out over the rustling wind and morning bird calls. "Identify yourself, traveller."

The man on foot raises his hands, smiles. "I'm unarmed but for my knife, good sir."

"It's all right," says Allaigna, her voice low and musical, honey to my ears. "I know him."

Chriani gives her a look that is so much that of a grumpy father I nearly laugh out loud. Allaigna shoulders past him and hurries down the road to meet Glaignen.

I can tell by Chriani's raised eyebrow that he wants to eavesdrop. He can't, but I can.

"Glaignen," Allaigna hisses as she gets nearer. "What are you doing here? And how did you find me?"

He gives his cheerful vulpine smile and cocks his head. "Why, I've been only a day's ride behind you most of this time. But when I heard your voice last night . . . I kept on through dark till I got here."

She shakes her head, puzzled. "If you were a day's ride away, how did you hear me?"

His grin widens as he reaches into his pack and pulls out a bowl I recognize. Nourd's. "Not so hard with this. And you're a lot easier to follow when you don't have *this*."

He drops something into the bowl. I focus hard, pulling my Sight closer, and see the blurry shape of Allaigna's pendant, resisting my scrying even as it sits quietly in the bowl.

Allaigna reaches out, cups the pendant in her hand, and then lets it go. "I told you, I don't want to be a seer."

"Then put the bowl in your pack and use it to wash your

dishes. But this …" He reties the pendant about her neck. She doesn't object. "This is bound to you. And it's safer on you than in someone else's hands. Even mine."

That is the last time for many years that I can easily scry Allaigna. But there are others around her, and by watching them, I can watch her. The balladeer, Kaelin, is easy to find, for she becomes the focus of the company's attention when they gather around cook-fires. All those eyes and ears intent upon her act like a lens, magnifying the vision. Kaelin's lover, Chriani, I have come to know over well these past decades. He is like a magnet for my Sight. And though Allaigna blurs and shimmers in the bowl when she passes close to them, I know she is there and safe. What's more, at Kaelin's elbow she is attaining as fine an apprenticeship in lore and music as I could hope for.

I never see the blood blade she took from her mother, and am relieved. I still believe she has it but that Chriani has convinced her of the sense in keeping it hidden. Hidden or not, it poses a danger to her, but it is still safer in her hands than in any other's. And for now, they are both safer in Chriani's care than in mine — a knowledge that galls me as I feel the concordance of futures nearing an apex here in quiet Teillai.

I watch for a long time on these evenings, enjoying vicariously the peace and camaraderie of the campfire, wishing I were there and not here, where chaos is bubbling beneath the surface calm.

§

Allaigna's Song: Chorale, *as well as the first two novels of the trilogy,* Overture *and* Aria, *are available from Pulp Literature Press and most booksellers.*

THE ARTISTS

BRONWYN SCHUSTER
Cover artist, Space Cat
Bronwyn was born near the Rocky Mountains and raised in the
Prairies. They now reside on the Gulf Islands in BC. Bronwyn
studied realism, portraiture, and figurative art at the Swedish
Academy of Realist Art and Illustration with Sam Weber and
Scott M Fischer at SmArt School. The art they create is a blend
between magical fiction and everyday realism, infused with a
little humour. Bronwyn's work utilizes multiple mediums, from
oil paint, gouache, graphite, and ink to digital media, and has
won awards such as Saskatchewan's Premier's Centennial Art
Scholarship and the coveted Art Renewal Center Scholarship.

DANTE LUIZ
Artist, 'Sap & Seed'
Dante Luiz (@dntlz on Twitter) is an illustrator, art director for
Strange Horizons, and occasional writer from southern Brazil.
He is the interior artist for *Crema*, forthcoming from Dark Horse,
and his work with comics has also appeared in anthologies like
Wayward Kindred, *Mañana*, and *Shout Out*, among others.

He lives in southern Brazil with his writer wife, H. Pueyo. They
have collaborated on many comics, most frequently for *Filthy Figments*.
To them, working together feels only natural, as they love creating
stories (it's how they met in the first place) and they're mad about

each other, so it's combining business with pleasure. You might find them on Twitter as @dntlz and @hachepueyo, where they might not post that much, but they always update the accounts with their new projects and creations.

MEL ANASTASIOU
In-house illustrator
Mel Anastasiou loves drawing for *Pulp Literature* because she loves the stories she illustrates. She draws in black and white, working from imagination and inspired by details from Renaissance compositions. You can find illustrations, writing tips, and news about her books and novellas at melanastasiou.wordpress.com, and see more of her artwork on Facebook at Bird and Branch Artwork.

HALL OF FAME

These are the heroes — the Patrons and Pulp Literati whose monthly support helped bring you this issue. Please lift your glasses and give them a rousing cheer!

The Shareholders
Rapscallion

The Brewers
Robin McGillveray
A Bursewicz

The Landlords
Isabel Cushey
Dana Tye Rally

The Innkeepers
Ada Maria Soto
Margot Landels
Ev Bishop
Shannon Saunders
Roger & Anne Anastasiou
Kevin Harris
Gillian Gardiner
Megan Shaw
Susan Jackson
Meghan Dahl
The Cicerones
Elsa Carruthers

The Bartenders
Alana Krider
Richard Gropp
Ron Graves

Kristen Mah
Robert Bose
Victoria McAuley
Dave Wayne
Scott F Gray
Michelle Balfour
Abigail Bruce
Vernice Dietra Malik
Katriona Greenmoor
AD Bane
KT Wagner
Michael Weckworth
Deepthi Atukorala
Margot Spronk
Margaret Elliott
Peter Halasz
Bjarne Hansen
Leny Wagner
Kain Stewart
Chris Olee
kc dyer
Kimberley Aslett
Jan Fagan
Ken Oakes
Brighton Hugg
Alexa Benzaid-
Williams
Bryan Moose
Maureen Cooke

Lorna Keach
Katja Rammer

The Regulars
CC Humphreys
Marta Salek
Rina Piccolo
Emily Lonie
Jenny Blackford
Jain Cairns
Akemi Art
BC
Meredith Frazier
Catherine Levinson
Vera
Charity Tahmaseb
Alexander Langer
Marilyn Holt
Risa Wolf
Barbara Pengelly
David Perlmutter
Christine McCullough
Ishbel Newstead

The Clientele
Ray Hsu
Melissa Hudson

If you would like to join the ranks of these worthies, you can become a patron on Patreon at patreon.com/pulplit or join the Pulp Literati through our website at pulpliterature.com/join-pulp-literati/.

Have you heard?

Pulp Literature has a podcast!

Our podcast **The Pulp Lit Pulpit** is available on Podbean. The episodes are filled with editor advice, exclusive author interviews, and serialized story-time instalments from *Allaigna's Song: Overture* and *Stella Ryman and the Fairmount Manor Mysteries*.

Each episode has a limited lifespan of about eight to twelve weeks, after which it's gone! The episodes are available for download so you can save them for when you want to hear them most. **Find the latest episodes here:** pulpliterature.podbean.com

https://pulpliterature.com   @pulpliteraturepress

MARKETPLACE

Books

Advent *by Michael Kamakana* · We thought we knew what the aliens wanted. Think again. · pulpliterature.com/advent

Allaigna's Song: Chorale *by JM Landels* · · The long-awaited conclusion to the bestselling *Allaigna's Song* trilogy. · pulpliterature.com/allaignas-song

The Extra: A Monument Studios Mystery *by Mel Anastasiou* · Extra Frankie Ray gets her big break on the Silver Screen, until Murder steals the scene. pulpliterature.com/the-extra

The Labours of Mrs Stella Ryman: Further Fairmount Mysteries *by Mel Anastasiou* · Trapped in a down-at-the-heels care home. You'd be cranky too. · pulpliterature.com/stella-ryman-and-the-fairmount-manor-mysteries

What the Wind Brings *by Matthew Hughes* · Winner of the 2020 Endeavour Award · pulpliterature.com/product-category/novels/matthew-hughes

The Writer's Boon Companion *by Mel Anastasiou* · Thirty Days Towards an Extraordinary Volume · pulpliterature.com/subscribe/the-bookstore

Bookstores

Book Warehouse · 632 Broadway W, Vancouver, BC V5Z 1G1 · 604-872-5711 bookwarehouse.ca

Myth Hawker Travelling Bookstore · Canadian authors · Canadian content · small & independent press · mythhawker.ca

Phoenix On Bowen · 992 Dorman Rd, Bowen Island, BC V0N 1G0 · 604-947-2793

Village Books & Coffee House · 130-12031 First Ave, Richmond, BC V7E 3M1 · 604-272-6601 · villagebooks@shaw.ca

Western Sky Books · 2132-2850 Shaughnessy St, Port Coquitlam, BC V3C 6K5 · 604-461-5602 · store.westernskybooks.com

White Dwarf / Dead Write Books · 3715 10th Ave W, Vancouver, BC V6R 2G5 · 604-228-8223 · whitedwarf@deadwrite.com

Conferences & Events

Word on the Lake · May 2022 · Salmon Arm, BC · wordonthelakewritersfestival.com

When Words Collide · August 2022 Calgary, AB · whenwordscollide.org

Wine Country Writers' Festival · Sept. 2022 · winecountrywriters-festival.ca

Surrey International Writers' Conference October 2022 · siwc.ca

HELP WANTED?

If you are a new writer, or a writer with a
troublesome manuscript,
EVENT's **Reading Service for Writers**
may be just what you need.

Manuscripts will be edited by one of EVENT's editors and receive an
assessment of 700-1000 words, focusing on such aspects of craft as
voice, structure, rhythm and point of view.

---

eventmagazine.ca

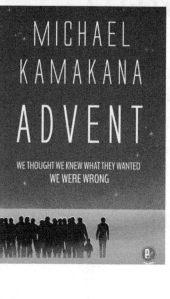

Magazines

Amazing Stories · Back in print!
amazingstories.com

The Digest Enthusiast · Digests
past & present plus new genre fiction
larquepress.com

EVENT Magazine · Poetry & prose
eventmagazine.ca

Geist Ideas + Culture · Made in Canada
geist.com

Mystery Weekly Magazine
The cutting edge of short mystery fiction
www.mysteryweekly.com

Neo-opsis · Canadian magazine of
science fiction based in Victoria, BC ·
neo-opsis.ca

OnSpec · The Canadian magazine of
the fantastic · onspecmag.wordpress.com

Polar Borealis · Paying market for new Canadian SF&F writers & artists · polarborealis.ca

Room Magazine · Literature, Art &
Feminism since 1975 · roommagazine.com

Printing & Publishing

First Choice Books/Victoria Bindery
Book printing & binding · graphic
design · eBooks · marketing materials
1-800-957-0561 · firstchoicebooks.ca

Writing Resources

Dreamers Creative Writing · Workshops,
residencies, contests & more! · www.
dreamerswriting.com

Quit the Day Job · A school for
writers from Pulp Literature Press
pulpliterature.com/quit-the-day-job

The Writers' Lodge on Bowen Island
The Muse retreats for writers · pulpliter-
ature.com/calendar-of-events/retreats/

The Labours of Mrs Stella Ryman
Further Fairmount Manor Mysteries

When the machineries of institution fail to protect Fairmount Manor, octogenarian amateur sleuth Mrs Stella Ryman rolls up her fleece jacket sleeves to ferret out a thief, investigate a gun-toting resident, set right a mishandled investigation of a man's death, pursue spectres and footpads walking at midnight, and discover Thelma Hu's long-lost fortune.

Book II of the Fairmount Manor Mysteries
by Mel Anastasiou, available now
from Pulp Literature Press

PULPLITERATURE.COM/STELLA-RYMAN
ISBN (PRINT): 978-1-988865-11-9
ISBN (EBOOK): 978-1-988865-12-6

CONTESTS

Pulp Literature runs four annual contests for poetry, flash fiction, and short stories. For contest guidelines, prizes, and entry fees, see pulpliterature.com/contests.

The Bumblebee Flash Fiction Contest
Contest opens: 1 January 2022
Deadline: 15 February 2022
Winner notified: 15 March 2022
Winner published: Issue 35, Summer 2022
Prize: $300

The Magpie Award for Poetry
Contest opens: 1 March 2022
Deadline: 15 April 2022
Winner notified: 15 May 2022
Winner published: Issue 36, Autumn 2022
Prize: $500

The Hummingbird Flash Fiction Prize
Contest opens: 1 May 2022
Deadline: 15 June 2022
Winner notified: 15 July 2022
Winner published: Issue 37, Winter 2023
Prize: $300

The Raven Short Story Contest
Contest opens: 1 September 2022
Deadline: 15 October 2022
Winner notified: 15 November 2022
Winner published: Issue 38, Spring 2023
Prize: $300

ℬECOME A PATRON OF PULP LITERATURE

By supporting *Pulp Literature* on Patreon with $2 or more per month, you will be laying the foundation for a secure future for the magazine, as well as ensuring that you never miss an issue! Your subscription includes four big issues of short stories, novellas, poetry, comics, and novel excerpts, delivered to your door or electronic mailbox each year. **Find us at patreon.com/pulplit**

If you prefer to subscribe through our website, go to pulpliterature.com/subscribe.

Or you can send a cheque with the form below to
Subscriptions, Pulp Literature Press, 21955 16 Ave, Langley BC, V2Z 1K5, Canada

....

Don't miss an issue!

❑ **Send me 2 years (8 issues) at the special rate of $90** (save $30)*
❑ **Send me 1 year (4 issues) for $50** (save $10)*
❑ **Send me 2 years of digital issues for $30** (save $9.92)
❑ **Send me 1 year of digital issues for $17.50** (save $2.47)

Name: _____
Address: _____
City: _____ Prov. / State: _____
Postal code: _____ Country:_____
Email: _____

❑ Payment enclosed
❑ Bill me
❑ New
❑ Renewal

Make cheques payable in Canadian funds to Pulp Literature Press. Include email address for digital editions and Paypal billing, or subscribe at www.pulpliterature.com.

*for postage outside Canada add $20 per year in North America or $36 per year overseas.

Made in the USA
Middletown, DE
23 July 2022

69917479R00117